P9-DNE-415

RICHARD PAUL EVANS

THE
CAROUSEL

A Novel

BOOKSPAN LARGE PRINT EDITION

Simon & Schuster
NEW YORK   LONDON   TORONTO
SYDNEY   SINGAPORE

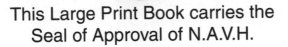

This Large Print Book carries the
Seal of Approval of N.A.V.H.

SIMON & SCHUSTER
Rockefeller Center
1230 Avenue of the Americas
New York, NY 10020

Simon & Schuster and colophon are registered trademarks
of Simon & Schuster, Inc.

Designed by Bonni Leon-Berman

Manufactured in the United States of America

ISBN 0-7432-0090-X

Acknowledgments

I would like to acknowledge those who helped make this book (and my life) possible: my wife, Keri, for her undying patience and putting up with "the life." Laurie Liss, my friend and confidante. Sydny Miner. Again, it has been a joy working with you, Love. Brandi Anderson. Thank you for your many contributions to this book, and, especially, your encouragement. Krista Story, for loving crowd control. David Rosenthal. Carolyn Reidy. Melissa Milsten. Isolde C. Sauer. Jackie Seow. Elizabeth Hayes. Gary Stephenson (Director of Public Affairs, Johns Hopkins University). Dr. Frank Herlong (Dean of Student Affairs, Johns Hopkins University). Dr. Horace Liang (Johns Hopkins Department of

Acknowledgments

Emergency Medicine). Dr. Richard Ferre. Dian Tucker (Holladay Health Care). Kim Macfarlane (Administrator, Holladay Health Care). Joann Furbish (Director of Nursing, Holladay Health Care). Rev. George Davich (St. Vincent Catholic Parish, Salt Lake City). My friend, Jonathan Linton. Thank you for listening. You changed this story. The crew: Jennifer Bagley, Lisa May, Tawna Spoor, Becky Avery, and Judy Schiffman. Thank you, Jennifer, for sharing so much. And, especially, to my loyal readers who make the publication of my books possible. Thank you for your letters and e-mail. Thank you for reading and sharing.

Though this story is fictional, the character of the waitress, Hallie, was inspired, in part, by the life of a real individual—an incredible woman by the name of Janie Webster.

Janie has written a book about her own experience entitled *Fingernail Moon*, published by Doubleday. It is the true story of a woman who gave up everything to save her daughter's life. I thank Janie for

ACKNOWLEDGMENTS

her example of courage and love as well as her editorial assistance.

SHARE: Pregnancy and Infant Loss Support, Inc., offers support to parents who have lost a baby through miscarriage, stillbirth, or early infant death. For more information please call: 1-800-821-6819.

To Allyson-Danica

Contents

THE
CAROUSEL

To dream is to hope.
To hope is to live.

MICHAEL KEDDINGTON'S JOURNAL

Prologue

There are years of our lives that pass like strangers on a busy streetwalk—as quickly forgotten as encountered. Then there are those years whose events cling to us as tenaciously as relatives to a rich uncle's will. Nineteen eighty-nine was such a year.

Globally, it was a remarkable year. The Berlin Wall fell. Solidarity swept to victory in Poland. And while the first free election was held in Russia, a half-million Chinese students protested for democracy on Tiananmen Square.

Still, it is my experience that the most profound events of our lives rarely end up on the six o'clock news. They are the journeys walked in solitude, to triumph or fail in the shadow of obscurity.

I took the first step of many journeys that year—some that I walk to this day. It was when I learned that love cannot exist without forgiveness and that faith is more enduring than understanding. And I learned more about loss than I ever cared to.

Indelibly linked to that year was the dream I had before everything went crazy. The dream of a carousel.

I have always been fascinated by dreams. As a teenager I once kept a journal of my dreams for an entire summer. They were, to my way of thinking, as meaningless as they were bizarre, though I'm sure they'd provide a banquet of pathological tidbits for a psychologist.

I am not alone in my fascination with dreams. From the ancient Babylonian dream books to the writings of Freud, dreams have played an important role in history. Muhammadanism and Buddhism were born of dreams, and Christianity is not without their influence. Some cultures believe that dreams are the walk of the soul, going so far as to punish a man for the crimes committed in his dreams.

There are those who believe dreams are prophetic—portents of future events. It is a theory not without its evidences. Abraham Lincoln dreamt of his own death. A few days before his assassination he told a friend that he dreamt there was a crowd gathered in the White House around a coffin. "Who has died in the White House?" he asked a soldier. "The President," was his answer. "He was killed by an assassin!" A loud burst of grief from the crowd woke him. He did not sleep the rest of that night. Three nights later he slept forever.

I don't know if there's any significance to the colors of dreams, but my carousel dream was not a vivid, Technicolor production; rather it was viewed in brown hues like an old-fashioned sepia photograph. In my dream, Faye, my girlfriend, sat next to me on a tuft of grass in front of an antiquated, steam-powered carousel. The carousel was large and elaborate with a canopy that pitched high like a circus tent. A pennant waved from its pinnacle. Around its circumference were beveled mirrors and gilt shields mounted with jester-heads and cherubs. On its platform was a finely carved, richly painted menagerie of animals: horses, elephants, zebras, rabbits, camels, giraffes, and lions.

The carousel's organ music was nearly drowned out by the sounds of those that filled the ride: men wearing silk-banded boaters or derbies, women wearing shirt-waists and flowing tea gowns and great bouquets of hats, children dressed neatly in knickers and pinafores, all laughing and shrieking with fear and delight.

Faye suddenly left me, running off toward the crowd. She handed the carnival barker her ticket, then glanced back at me and smiled as the carousel slowed. She boarded its still-moving platform. The noise and motion rose. As she came around I waved to her. She was seated, sidesaddle, on a jeweled Arabian charger, her arm looped around the great brass pole that impaled the beast. With her free arm, she beckoned for me to join her.

As I approached, the carousel made a complete revolution. As Faye's horse came around again, it was riderless. I looked to the carnival man for an explanation, but he offered none. On its next revolution, a stranger sat on the horse where Faye had been. I shouted at the carnival man to stop the ride.

"It doesn't stop," he said.

"But she's gone."

"Sometimes that happens."

I watched as the carousel continued to spin, the cheerful strains from the organ mocking my agony.

"Will I see her again?"

The man looked back over his shoulder, following the rise and fall of the animals with his eyes, then finally turned to me. "I suppose that's up to you."

It was August 24 when I had the dream. At the time I was employed as a nursing assistant at the Arcadia Care Facility—a home for the elderly, located a mile up Ogden Canyon in northern Utah. Much had already happened that year. In January I had been falsely accused of beating one of the residents, an elderly black man by the name of Henri McCord. I was jailed for a time, and, not surprisingly, was relieved of my job pending an investigation. It was spring when I stood before a jury to be acquitted of the charge. It was during that trial that I lost the woman who had helped me through it; Esther Huish, a beautiful and sad elderly woman whom I met at the Arcadia. It was her emerald engagement ring that I had given Faye when I asked her to marry me. Though I was immediately offered my job back, I did not return to the facility until July.

I remember the exact date of the carousel dream because it was two nights before Faye was to leave for Baltimore for medical school. It was the beginning of a journey that would change the course of both of our lives. It was also the night Della died.

CHAPTER ONE

Della

There was another death tonight at the Arcadia. Della Estelle Gifford. There were no family or friends at her side, only us employees. As many times as I have experienced such lonely passings I still do not understand how, with so many people on this planet, so many die alone.

MICHAEL KEDDINGTON'S JOURNAL

Arcadia Care Facility. Ogden, Utah.

There was a moon that night, a pale crescent that hung low above the canyon and shone weakly into the dying woman's window. Della's was not a spectacular death, if any death can be described as spectacular. She made several attempts to blow out a flameless birthday candle, then reclined in her bed, rubbed the translucent skin of her liver spot–flecked forehead, and mumbled something about Errol Flynn. Twenty minutes later she gasped twice, then died.

There was no family present at her passing, just the three of us, all paid to be there: Sharon Holt, Brent Griffin, and myself, sitting around her in that dimly lit fourteen-foot square. Sharon was the nurse on duty and I was glad for that. Sharon knew death—more so than any of us. In her twenty-year tenure as a hospice nurse Sharon had eased the passage of the dying hundreds of times, holding their hands and administering pain relief as they took their final breaths. Likely more times than she could remember, except I would wager that she could remember; could put a name to each resident, maybe even the time their vitals failed. She was as compassionate as an angel. "No one dies alone," she would say, and she saw to it that no one on her watch did unless a resident stole off in their sleep. I was grateful that she had been at Esther's side when she passed away.

Without word Sharon pressed her index finger over Della's wrist, then placed a stethoscope to her chest, straining to hear a heartbeat. Then she checked her watch and recorded the time. It was Brent who was the first to break the silence.

"She died on her birthday."

Brent's comment was meant as a joke. I shook my head. Sharon ignored him completely, something she did instinctively.

It was no great coincidence that Della died on her birthday, as every day was Della's birthday. As dementia had conquered her ninety-six-year-old mind, two things took root and refused to be extricated—the first was that every day she woke to her birthday. Della didn't actually remember the date of her birthday or even the current day—just that it was *the* day.

In truth, we didn't know what day Della's birthday was. A quick glance at her resident record would have enlightened us, but no one ever bothered to do it. Some delusions, even in the clear-minded, are best left unchallenged.

We had a candle, Della's candle, that we would put into her dessert each day at suppertime, be it yellow cake or a green square of gelatin. I once saw it stuck into a scoop of mashed potatoes. It didn't matter to Della.

Because of her oxygen tank, fire was not allowed near her, so one candle lasted indefinitely. The eternal flameless. Each evening one of us would take Della her meal with the candle affixed, delivered with a hasty verse of "Happy Birthday," and Della would beam and sometimes join in, her voice as inconstant as a cell phone in a mountain pass. Then she would smile and clap her hands together and say in a quavering voice, "Thank you for remembering."

"Thirty today, Della?"

At this she would bring her hand to her chest and laugh as hysterically as her frail frame allowed. When the last of her chuckles had subsided, we would ask, "Is Errol going to make it this year?" She would suddenly frown and say, "No, Errol is in Hollywood. He's making another picture-show, you know. He won't be coming today."

That was the other peculiar aspect of Della's dementia. She believed she and Errol Flynn had been married for thirty-something years. In all that time he never once made it to her birthday. Sometimes she'd cuss him out, but she'd as quickly forgive him, vocally reminding all present (even if it was only herself) that it is a husband's role to provide and Errol was a fine provider and had many fans that proved a considerable distraction. "One must take the bad with the good," she would say.

A newly hired orderly (I don't remember her name; she didn't last long) once took it on herself to correct Della's delusion. She informed Della that Errol Flynn was not her husband and had been married to three women in all, fathering children with each of them. Also that he had died thirty years previous. At first Della would not hear the heresy, but after several weeks, the orderly apparently had some success in convincing her. Della became sullen and despondent. After a week of this I decided that I couldn't bear it any longer and went in and told her that she had been lied to by a jealous orderly who was angry because Errol refused to sign an autograph for her the last time he came by. I told her that Errol had called with his regrets for missing her birthday, but would be in town soon and wanted her to save him some cake if it wasn't too much trouble. She was happy again after that.

I was genuinely saddened at Della's

passing. Sharon, as resident nurse, pro-
nounced Della dead, then phoned the
house physician and obtained a release for
the body while Brent and I gave her a bed
bath and changed her gown. About an hour
later two men from the mortuary arrived.
They carted her body off enclosed in a faux
velvet bag on a gurney. We saw to it that
such things were done as discreetly as possible. A death caused a curious reaction at
the Arcadia, a peculiar combination of
melancholy and envy. At times roommates
of the departed became morose and refused to eat and we would have to put
them on special watch.

I stripped the sheets from Della's bed. In
the morning, housekeeping would sterilize
the room in preparation for its next tenant.
The Arcadia was only a thirty-bed facility
and there was always someone waiting to
get in.

It was nearly eleven o'clock and the
home slept. The common-area lights were
dimmed or turned off, and the hallways
were lit by exit signs and staggered fluores-
cents.

Night is not especially kind to the elderly infirm. In the quiet darkness they would often wake disoriented or afraid. Some would shout out for someone to help them or call for a long-deceased spouse. Some would groan incessantly. Though I was used to it, I remember my first night shift. I thought the place sounded like a haunted house. It would scare children, I thought. Some adults too.

Most of the residents went to bed around seven-thirty, after dinner, though some of them did not wait to finish their meals before falling asleep. We would wheel them up from the dining room and lift them into their beds.

The most notable exception to the bed-time routine was Hazel. Hazel was as nocturnal as a possum. She had been a pharmacist for more than fifty years and was programmed for the graveyard shift. Dressed in overalls and white canvas sneakers, she would push her aluminum walker up and down the halls, inevitably settling at the nurses' station. She believed that she was more employee than resident and would refer to the other residents as "them crazy old farts" with deliberate self-distancing.

At least once a night she'd talk about her sons (They grew up mean. It was her own fault; she never disciplined them), ask to check on her money in the Arcadia's safe to be sure someone hadn't absconded with it—an event she fully expected—or ask for a case-by-case review of the residents' medicine charts. When we were not at the station she would sit near the counter where she would watch the call light board with the intensity of a Tijuana cabdriver eyeing a traffic light. The moment a light would blink she would start shouting, "Hey, isn't someone going to get that?! Don't neglect them. Do I have to do everything around here?"

Though Hazel was our most consistent night walker, she was not our only one. There was Eva. At least twice a week Eva would wake from a sound sleep and make for the exit, intent on walking home. Our explanation that New Jersey is an intolerably long walk from Utah could not dissuade her in the least. Though she moved slowly and rarely got past the nurses' station, one night she slipped off unnoticed. She was discovered by a motorist a block down the canyon in her nightgown. We installed an alarm on the stairwell door the next day.

Then there was "Buzzsaw Raymond." Raymond had sleep apnea which triggered the loudest snores I had ever heard. Snores that could wake even Brent. Raymond burned through roommates nearly as fast as we could move them in. It was a problem that vexed the Arcadia's greatest minds until one of the CNAs thought to move Howard in with Raymond and solved the problem. Howard was deaf.

My coworker, Brent Griffin, was another hallmark of the night shift. Hiring Brent ("the Griff," he called himself) was an act of desperation on the part of the Arcadia. Like most care facilities for the elderly, the Arcadia had a high rate of employee turnover. Brent had been hired on a month before my return, during a drought of applicants—a decision Helen, the Arcadia's director, questioned or rued each and every day of his employment. He had been assigned with Sharon and me to the second floor, and Helen still occasionally apologized to me for that. Brent was lazy, and though there were times all of us wanted to beat him, he was also amusing, which is worth something on a night shift.

Brent was a caricature of sorts, a man barely afloat in the murky waters of male self-doubt, forever bent on proving his manhood, usually with stereotypical manifestations of machismo. He had long sideburns and a scraggly bush of hair on his chin which he thought was cool. His weekly tales of female conquest, which he shared with any and all who would endure them—including the less coherent residents—were, when believable, more pathetic than inspiring. Sharon once called him "a man who had been pantsed one too many times in high school."

Ten minutes to eleven I found Brent in the break room. He was sprawled out on the couch, his eyes were closed, and one leg stuck straight out, propped up by the couch's arm. It hadn't been difficult guessing where to find him. Brent worked the usual night shift, from six to two, and despite his schedule, he never really cut back his daily activities, which we all paid for in the later hours of his shift.

I shook his foot. "Wake up, Brent."

One eyelid lifted above a grimace. "What?" he said groggily.

"I need you to finish the west wing."

"Huh?" He looked up at me. "I thought you were doing it."

"I'm off early tonight."

He groaned. "Is someone else coming in?"

"Not until midnight." Just like every night for the last two months, I thought.

He took an exaggerated breath then lifted himself to a sitting position. "Yeah, I'll do it." When he gained more consciousness he asked, "You workin' tomorrow?"

"No. I've got the day off. Faye leaves Saturday."

"I finally met her the other night. She was looking for you. Wish she was looking for me. Don't get mad or nothing, 'cause I didn't know she was yours, but I made a move on her. Laid down one of the Griff's sweetest lines."

I could only imagine it. The whole of Brent's five-foot-six, hundred-and-twenty-five-pound frame leaning against the front counter emphasizing each syllable of his come-on with a tilt of his head or raised eyebrow, "Hey, baby, ain't it a shame. All those curves and me with no brakes." It was probably all Faye could do to not burst out in laughter. Or beat him senseless. I grinned at the thought of it.

". . . where's she off to?"

"Baltimore. She's studying medicine at Johns Hopkins."

Brent's mouth pursed. "Johns Hopkins. Man, I'm hanging out at the wrong bars. Those looks and a paycheck. How long will she be gone?"

"Four long years."

"Gotta be hating that, man. You guys like engaged?"

"No," I lied. "We're promised."

"Whoa. That's like four years of celibacy.

Or sneaking around. Guys like us have our seeds to sow."

I cringed at being lumped into the same category as Brent.

". . . 'course that blade cuts both ways," he continued. "You can bet all those slicky-boy doctors are gonna be working her like a bad leg. You can't trust doctors. They're all just in it for the money and the chicks."

"I don't think Faye's in it for either."

"If that babe were mine she wouldn't be going nowhere."

"Probably why she isn't yours," I said.

He bobbed his head as he stood, though I doubt he knew what I meant. Brent was more stupid than malicious.

"Why ain't you with her tonight?"

"Her girlfriends are throwing her a party. Girls-only deal."

"Oh," he said, bending the word as if he knew something about such functions that I didn't.

I watched him saunter over to the coffee machine in slow motion and knew there would be residents neglected. "I'll finish the first half of the hall before I go," I said.

Brent took his coffee and sat back into the couch, his legs spread apart and his head back. "No problem, man."

CHAPTER TWO

The Chapel of Eternal Bliss

Summer is a fever of sorts.
Hot and deceptive.
Like falling in love.

MICHAEL KEDDINGTON'S JOURNAL

Faye was perennially summer. More than bronze-skinned and barefoot, she was the warm nights of the season, the hot breeze that caressed my hair, dampened my brow, and filled each breath. Summer and all its reckless promise. I did not work much that summer. After what I had been put through with the false accusation and trial, Helen, the Arcadia's director, was overly accommodating and I delayed my return for as long as I could afford to be unemployed. I started back in mid-July, six weeks before Faye left.

We both knew that it would be our last carefree summer together. We spent those days constructing our dreams of a life together, clinging to each hour as tightly as a mountain climber holds to the rock face of a vertical climb, tethering our dreams and futures to our promises. But summer always ends. And in the end, promises weren't enough.

It was nearly midnight when I arrived home from work. To my surprise, Faye's BMW was parked in the driveway. She was inside her car listening to the radio, her eyes closed and her head swaying with the music. I knocked on her window and startled her. She shut off the engine and opened the door, laughing at herself, her hand on her chest.

"I hope you know CPR. You nearly stopped my heart."

"You stop my heart every time I look at you," I said.

She smiled at this and got out of the car. I brushed her hair back from her face then kissed her. "What are you doing here?"

"Waiting for my man. The party was at a dance club. Everyone started picking up guys, so I decided to go get mine."

We kissed again. Then she reached back into her car and pulled out a plastic sack.

"Look what I brought. Snelgrove's ice cream."

We went inside and made caramel sundaes, then came back out and sat on the porch steps to eat. Summer was waning and the air was cool but not yet uncomfortable.

There's not much of a view from my front porch, day or night; the silhouette of my neighbor's Bondo-patched El Camino, a row of low-income tract houses with faded canopy awnings, aged aluminum siding, and burned-up lawns, all beneath a backdrop of power lines leading to the nearby UP&L substation. But I wasn't looking around much. The view couldn't get much better than Faye. I held her and we kissed, our lips sticky from the ice cream. We didn't talk about her impending departure. We didn't need to, as it found its way into every look and nuance. It was the punctuation at the end of each sentence, the separation at the end of every kiss.

By one-thirty Faye could barely keep her eyes open, so we unwound ourselves from each other and I walked her to her car.

"What time tomorrow?" I asked.

"It's already tomorrow," she said. "Sunup. I want every minute with you I can squeeze out of a day."

"What's the agenda?"

"About a million errands and . . ." she hesitated. "A shoe store."

I grimaced.

"I'm sorry. I'll make it up to you. There's someplace special I want to take you."

"Where?"

"You'll see."

Faye climbed into her car and I stood in the driveway until she turned from my street. Five minutes later I fell in bed with my clothes on. And I dreamed of a carousel.

As promised, Faye was back at dawn, checklist in hand. She had a lengthy list of things she needed to get or exchange before she left. We spent the morning running errands, which included an excruciating hour at a shoe store. To this day I believe it was really a litmus test of sorts, a final affirmation of the depth of my love. A man who spends more than thirty minutes at a shoe store is about as faithful as a woman can or should hope for.

Faye's mood changed with the hour and by noon she had become sullen. That's when she told me about the special place she had promised to take me. Summerset Park.

Summerset was one of Ogden's older parks. I had been there only once before, the first year my mother and I came to Utah. I had not been back since.

Faye and I drove to the west side of the park, where there was a small pond with paddleboats, a miniature Ferris wheel, and a carousel. I parked the car. Faye asked me to pop the trunk, which I did, and she went around and brought out of it a large sack. I asked her what was inside of it and she just said, "You'll see."

We bought hotdogs from a park vendor, loaded them down with mustard and sweet onion, then I followed Faye to a park bench on the side of the carousel that was shadowed by elm. It was a Friday after-noon and the park was quiet except for a handful of joggers and power walkers and a few solitary men and women in business attire who escaped to the park at their lunch break. A sign hung on a chain outside the carousel denoting that the attraction was closed.

We ate for a while, then Faye lifted the crinkled sack and said, "All right, open your present. I'm sorry it's not wrapped."

"What is it?"

"Open it and you'll see."

"I mean, what's it for?"

"It's your birthday present. I know it's early, but since I won't be here . . ." Her voice trailed off as if it pained her to speak of it.

I opened the bag. Inside was a Coach leather briefcase. I held it admiringly at arm's length. "This is really nice."

"A lawyer should have a nice briefcase. You can use it for school in the meantime."

I set it back in its wrappings. "Thank you." I kissed her, then said, "Imagine a doctor and a lawyer under the same roof. If I'm sick you can take care of me."

She grinned. "And if I'm not a good wife you can sue me for malpractice."

I grinned.

"Lawyers don't have their own version of a Hippocratic oath, do they?"

"Not that I know of."

"My dad says it's a shame that ninety-nine percent of the attorneys are giving the other one percent a bad name."

I smiled wryly. I hadn't even started law school and the insults had already begun. Faye set her drink under the bench, then shifted away from me and leaned her head back into my lap with her eyes closed, allowing her face to gather all the sun's rays not eclipsed by my body.

"When my dad first started at McKay-Davis he used to drop Jayne and me off here on Saturday afternoons. He'd give us each a roll of quarters and then go to the hospital to do research or whatever, while my mom had her friends over for bridge. Jayne was too short to reach the pedals on the paddleboats and too afraid of the Ferris wheel, so we would ride the carousel until our quarters were gone.

Our first time here we went through the rolls in about two hours and then we had to just sit around and wait until he came back. So the next time we decided that we would make the quarters last by taking turns; one of us would ride while the other would watch and wave every time it'd come around. We would sit at this very bench." She smiled in remembrance. "I still come here a lot. Whenever life gets overwhelming I just sit here and watch it go around. It takes me back to when the most difficult decision I had was figuring out how to make the quarters last until Dad came back."

I suddenly remembered the dream from the night before. "I had a dream last night that I was sitting with you by a carousel."

Faye's eyes opened and she raised a hand to shield her eyes from the sun. "What kind of dream?"

"We were looking at this old carousel and you climbed on it. When I went to join you, you were gone."

"Gone where?"

"I don't know. Where'd you go?"

She smiled at the question. "I went to find you, of course."

I looked back up at the carousel. "I think carousels are kind of frightening."

"What could be frightening about a carousel?"

I pointed toward one of the menagerie animals. "Look at that thing. What is it? Half fish, half horse, it's enough to give a kid nightmares."

"It's a hippocampus," Faye said.

I looked down at her. "How did you know that?"

"I read it somewhere." She smiled. "I like carousels."

We both ate for a while. Faye finished half of her hotdog, then, as she usually did, gave the rest of it to me.

"Maybe I like carousels because they're so constant. They always go to the same place. And they never change. You know, I've probably ridden every animal on there." The lightness of her expression faded to a more serious one. "Things are changing so much right now. I just feel like I want to hold on to something."

She looked into my eyes. "Especially to you."

She pulled the gold chain from beneath her blouse, exposing the emerald-and-gold engagement ring I had given her earlier that spring on our trip to Bethel. She caressed it for a moment, then took it off its chain and placed it on her ring finger, holding it out in front of her.

"I wish I didn't have to hide this." She looked up into my face. "Do you think we've done the right thing?" Before I could answer she said, "I'm not certain we've done the right thing. It feels like we've let my father make this decision for us."

Essentially he had. The doctor had drawn a line in the sand, forcing her to decide between me or school.

"If he knew you had that ring you wouldn't be leaving tomorrow."

"A tempting proposition," Faye said softly. She bit her lower lip, momentarily lost in thought, then she glanced up into my eyes and said, "Let's elope."

Initially I wasn't sure if she really meant it.

"Elope?"

"Yeah." She took my hand and set it on her waist. "We don't need to tell anyone."

"It's because I passed the shoe store test, isn't it?"

Faye was accustomed to my resorting to levity whenever I was anxious, and had learned to ignore it. "Why not, Michael?"

"Maybe," I said. "Maybe."

In truth there was nothing novel about the idea. I had considered the very thing pretty much every day that summer. But Faye's voice had given it a reality that my thoughts never dared. I looked down at the ground. There was a group of dandelions clustered near my feet. I kicked at them nervously. "Where does one go to elope?"

Faye glanced around the park then said, "Not Ogden. I don't think we could do it anywhere in Utah and keep it a secret."

Faye was right. We heard it everywhere we went, even in the most removed locales. "Are you Benjamin Murrow's daughter?" In addition to being an accomplished surgeon, Dr. Murrow was actively involved in Republican politics in a state that likes its Republicans, attested to by a row of porcelain elephants on a shelf in his office next to a framed picture of him with the governor. That and the fact that there were only two Murrows in the entire state, the other being Faye's uncle, it was likely that the interest of anyone in a government position would be piqued by her name. And just as likely that they would talk.

"We could drive up to Wyoming," I said. "Jackson Hole."

"I have relatives in Jackson Hole." She thought on it. "We'd have to go to Nevada."

"We'd never make it. Las Vegas is seven hours from here."

"I meant Wendover. There's that little wedding chapel where you drive into town. Across from the casino."

Wendover was a border town on the Nevada side of the Utah-Nevada line, only an hour and a half drive from Salt Lake City. It was an oasis from Utah's drinking and gambling laws—where Utahns went to purge the vice from their blood and the green from their wallets. The town's one claim to fame was that it was the location of the air base where the B-29 crews that dropped the bombs on Hiroshima and Nagasaki trained. The base had closed with the war, and the dusty Nevada skies that once droned from the sounds of the engines of the *Enola Gay* now droned from the sound of hapless gamblers returning to their homes a penny wiser and a dollar poorer; the ones who had nicknamed the place "Bend Over."

Looking back on that day it seems odd that we finished our lunch then went off to get married as casually as if it were just another errand to be crossed off Faye's list before she left town. We were soon back in Faye's BMW barreling west on I-80 toward the Utah-Nevada border.

The drive to Nevada is about as eventful as a New Year's Eve party at a convent. There was one thing to see. We passed the old Mercur Ranch exit; the same road we took to Bethel. We both looked out quietly over the pocked dirt road that cut across the mesquite-dotted plain. "We need to go back someday," Faye said.

Past the Oquirrh range, where its foot

dips into the brine of the Great Salt Lake, I-80 opened into the broad expanse of the Bonneville Salt Flats. It is one of the few places where one can see the curvature of the earth, the earth falling in chalky, alkali plains, as if the desert floor was stretched tight like the skin of a drum. We didn't say much during that ride. Not once did we really talk about what we were doing. Maybe because we were contemplative, but, more likely, because we were just plain scared. There's something about standing on the edge of a cliff that takes the words from you.

It took us about two hours to reach the state line, distinguishable in the distance by a large, animated neon sign of a cowboy pointing to the town's largest casino. Beneath the cowboy was listed an $8.95 all-you-can-eat prime rib dinner and the upcoming date of a keno tournament.

The courthouse was just west of the casino. It took less than a half hour to get the marriage license, which required only a driver's license, fifty dollars, and our signatures. It was more difficult getting my

video rental card. With our marriage certificate in hand we walked a block to the
chapel. In front of the building a sign read
in buzzing neon: *Wedding Chapel of Eternal Bliss.*

As we walked the gravel-lined sidewalk
to the chapel, about to take one of the most
important steps of our lives, I was thinking
that churches should not have neon signs.
Technically, it was not a church but a
chapel. Somewhere, in the semantics, I
suppose there's a difference.

No matter what you called it, it was an
ugly building, an alabaster-white, alu-
minum-paneled structure with a pediment
and porch stuck to its front entryway for
aesthetics. In reality, the addition was
about as aesthetically effective as mount-
ing a Rolls-Royce hood ornament to my
rusted-out Datsun. It was no more a church
than a Zamboni is a car. But, like I said, it
was a chapel not a church and, neon and
all, it served the measure of its creation.

I've often heard elopement spoken of ro-
mantically, but the truth was that I hurt for
Faye. She deserved more than a stealth

wedding. We had discussed weddings before and I was amazed at the bridal maga-
zine Faye had compiled in her head,
choreographing every detail of the day.
She knew it all, from the fabric of her
bridesmaids' dresses to the satin and lace
of her own bridal gown. Instead Faye wore
black pedal pushers with a red, rib-necked
cotton top. Later, when I asked her if she
was disappointed by the ceremony, she
only smiled and said that she got what
she wanted.

I opened the door for Faye then stepped
in behind her. The chapel's interior was a
single room, long and narrow and low
ceilinged. At the far end was a small
pedestal where vows were exchanged. The
pedestal was crimson, covered by the
same bright red carpet that filled the room.
To each side of the pedestal was a garish
white latticework with plastic ivy woven
through it. In front of each panel was a
gold-leafed wire-framed planter with bouquets of faux azaleas and chrysanthe-
mums. A small, round crystal-shard light
fixture hung from the middle of the room

above a few dozen metal chairs of the folding variety that had been painted white with uneven brush strokes.

A portly woman sat in the far corner of the room reading a tabloid, her feet propped up on an ottoman. Her large, scarlet hair twirled and raised to the heavens like the tiers of a wedding cake.

On a pine étagère to her side, an open can of Old Milwaukee sat next to a collection of cheap Hummel-like porcelains of children kissing or holding hands, artifacts that pass themselves off as decoration at dime stores and tourist traps: things that are best bought, and better sold, at garage sales. An oscillating fan passed across the woman and ruffled her paper.

Faye smiled nervously at me and I cleared my throat to get the woman's attention. The woman lowered her paper, exposing enough facial hair to warrant a razor's attention.

"What can I do for you folks?" she asked in a bass voice.

Faye answered, "We'd like to be married."

The woman pushed herself up from the chair and introduced herself.

"I'm Doreen, the minister here."

I suppose she seemed as much a minister to me as this place seemed a church, which was only appropriate. Faye just smiled. "I'm Faye. This is my fiancé, Michael."

"Pleased to know you both. Have you got your license?"

"Yes." I fumbled it from my shirt pocket. "Right here."

"Did you bring yourselves witnesses?"

Faye and I exchanged blank glances. The minister read the anxiety on our faces and waved a broad hand as if she were clearing a chalkboard. "Don't fret if you didn't. It's fifty for the ceremony. Seventy if I call in witnesses. Plus forty for yours truly. We can arrange for a Polaroid photograph for only twenty dollars more."

I did the math in my head. "Do you take out-of-state checks?"

"Sure do," she replied. "Ninety-nine nine percent of our business comes from Utah, honey."

Apparently witnesses were not hard to come by in a casino town. Upon my writing a check for a hundred and thirty dollars, the minister made two phone calls and in less than ten minutes two men walked into the room. They were familiar with the routine and both stopped to lift a clip-on tie from a rack on the way in, then took their places at their designated spots, one to each side of the pedestal, facing toward us. A chunky native American woman soon followed them, toting a Polaroid camera. Faye suddenly looked nervous as we walked to the pedestal, her hand woven in mine.

"I'll need your wedding license."

I released Faye's hand and handed the piece of paper to the minister. She glanced at it then looked back at me and said, "Do you have a ring?"

"I have it," Faye said. She quickly took it from its chain and offered it to her.

"Give it to him, honey," she said. Faye lightly blushed as she handed me the ring.

"I don't have a ring for you," Faye said softly.

"It's okay," I said. "One's enough."

"Have you written your own vows?"

"No, ma'am," I said. "This was kind of sudden."

"Well, I've got some here." She lifted a white leather Bible from the podium, taking a folded sheet from between its pages.

She cleared her throat. "We are gathered here in the sight of God and in the presence of these witnesses to join this man and this woman in the holy bonds of matrimony. Rather than to establish legal ownership of each other, marriage is the confirmation of a commitment already made to share happiness and trials encountered by each along the way. Those commitments are of a solemn nature, ones that are not to be taken lightly. As you have made this commitment with your hearts, let us now make them with your words." She lifted our marriage certificate. "Do you," she squinted at my name, "Michael Keddington, take," another squint and pause, "Faye Morrow to be your wife, to love and be considerate unto her from this day forth?"

"It's Murrow," I said.

"Excuse me?"

"Not Morrow," I said. "Murrow. Like the newsman."

She looked back down at our license. "Oh, Murrow. I'm sorry." She started again. "Do you, Michael Keddington, take Faye Murrow to be your wife, to love and be considerate unto her from this day forth?"

I looked into Faye's eyes, and as she stared back it suddenly became very real.

"Yes. I do."

"Do you, Faye Murrow, take Michael Keddington to be your husband, to love and be considerate unto him from this day forth?"

Her eyes were moist. She said, "I do."

The minister looked up from her sheet directly at me. "Repeat after me and then place the ring on her finger. 'I give you this symbol of my pledge for faithful love and remembrance of these vows.' " I repeated her words then slipped the ring on Faye's finger.

"Michael and Faye have come here as two and shall leave here as one, united by marriage, and may nothing in life come between them to sever this bond."

She cleared her throat, looking down from her book at us. "Please join hands. Both of them."

We were now standing squarely facing each other.

"With this joining of hands you take upon yourselves this new relationship of husband and wife. You have promised to love, honor, and cherish each other as such and now, in accordance with the laws of the State of Nevada and authority vested in me, I do hereby pronounce you Husband and Wife."

There was a flash at that moment as Faye and I gazed into each other's eyes. We leaned forward and kissed. It was electric.

We collected our photograph. Doreen signed our wedding certificate, then gave us a book of money-saving coupons donated by the casino. The two witnesses also shook our hands, then held their palms out to Doreen, who gave them each a ten-dollar bill. They hurried out muttering their congratulations as they left, though in their hurry, they sounded more like condolences.

In retrospect we were both a little dazed. We ate dinner at the casino, then briefly debated the merits of getting a room right there to spend our honeymoon night, but decided instead to return to Ogden and spend what time we had left at my place. It was either that or get up at three in the morning to drive back home. We stopped at a gas station on the edge of town, and Faye called to tell her mother that she would be spending the night at her friend Shandra's. Then she called Shandra to let her know of the sham, in the unlikely event one of Faye's parents called. Shandra was Faye's best friend and one of the few married ones that she'd kept in touch with after high school. Faye did not tell her that we had eloped, but it didn't matter. Shandra was experienced at covering for us.

When we arrived at my house, our house, I unlocked the door and lifted Faye across the threshold. It made her laugh.

"You're such a slave to tradition," she said. She went straight to the kitchen. I heard a cupboard door shut and she emerged with both hands concealed behind her back.

"You're grinning like a fool. What are you hiding?"

"You want tradition? I'll give you tradition." She threw two handfuls of rice at me. She started back to the kitchen for more and I grabbed her at the doorway and we fell onto the carpet, laughing. Then she rolled over on top of me. Her eyes were wild and a playful smile lit her face.

"You caught me. I'm yours."

"I think you caught me."

"I think you're right." We kissed, rolling over to our sides, our faces just inches apart.

"Welcome to your bridal suite, Mrs. Keddington. We have all the amenities of the finer domiciles. Running water—from real holes in the roof. Shag carpet from the sixties. A queen-size mattress on the floor."

"You have rice in your hair," she replied. While she picked at the grains she said, "I think it's all rather romantic."

"I suppose it's all in the eyes of the beholder," I said.

She pressed her nose against mine. "And what kind of eyes are those?"

"The most enchanting eyes I have ever gazed into."

"They better be the only eyes I ever catch you gazing into. I intend to keep you on a very short leash."

"It better be a very long one from Baltimore."

"Baltimore," she repeated softly. Faye began to unbutton my shirt. "We only have nine hours, Michael."

"Nine hours," I echoed.

"Nine hours," and she placed her finger over my lips and there was no more talk.

CHAPTER THREE
Home

Maybe it's a trait of the male gender, or maybe it's just me, but I never really considered what my marriage ceremony would be like—only the woman I wished to share it with. Faye is everything I hoped for. In Faye's love, I have found more than a friend and companion. I have found home.

MICHAEL KEDDINGTON'S JOURNAL

I didn't know, didn't care, the hour when Faye fell asleep in my arms. But I did not sleep. Holding this lovely, warm woman against me, I wanted to draw out each moment, to savor each rise and fall of her body, her face buried against my chest, her skin melting into mine. To hold on to what I knew must surely pass. The moment I closed my eyes it would be gone. Like the inverse of a dream.

If I could hold any moment of my life, to freeze it and relive it at will, it would be this one. Feeling Faye breathe next to me, listening to her sighs, it was all miraculous to me. Maybe it was just home that I felt at that moment. Home from the solitary journey I had seemed to travel as long as I had been. In Faye's embrace the alienation I felt from the world was gone. Exorcised or appeased, I'm not certain, for as familiar as it was to me, I still didn't know the nature of that particular demon. But something was different. Something deep inside me was changed. Healed.

I had never imagined that I could feel so close to anyone. I've never been very religious, but I have heard scripture recited about a man and a woman being joined as one. I now understood that to come together was less a physical act than a spiritual one. Two spirits forever bound. It was as real as any graft could be.

I woke around seven to Faye's kiss. She was kneeling over me in bed, her legs straddling my waist. She had already showered and her hair was damp and drawn back. She was wearing her pedal pushers and one of my T-shirts, which draped over her like a smock. Her ring again hung from the chain around her neck.

"So what now, cowboy? You woke with a wife."

I smiled and pulled her warm body back into mine. My voice was raspy. "I think I need to sell this place and move to Baltimore."

"I think you're right." Faye caressed my stubbled cheek with her hand. "I've never woken to a man."

"How was it?"

"I liked it." After another minute she said, "Maybe we should wait until I'm done with my first year."

"For what?"

"For you to move out to Baltimore."

"I don't think I can be away from you that long."

She sighed. "I know I can't be away from you that long. Let's see how this quarter goes."

A moment later the phone rang. Faye looked at me anxiously. "Don't worry," I said, "I won't tell him that you're here." I rolled over and lifted the receiver.

"Hello. Oh, hi. Yeah, just a moment." I handed Faye the phone. "It's Shandra."

Faye took the phone. "Hi."

Shandra said something that caused

Faye to smile then laugh. "Okay, thanks." She handed the phone back to me to hang up.

"What did she want?"

Faye nestled back into me. "Dad just called for me over there. Shandra told him I was in the shower."

"That made you laugh?"

"No, it was her commentary about finding me here in the morning." She smiled and said, "This web of deceit we weave. I've never told so many lies in my life and it's all your fault. I'm going to have to do a couple thousand Hail Marys and Our Fathers."

"As long as those lies aren't to me," I said.

"To you I'm transparent." She arched back. "I have to go," she moaned. She raised up to her knees, then stood. She stepped over me and walked to my bedroom door, where she sat back down to lace her shoes. I pulled on my jeans, climbed out of bed, and went to her. She finished tying her shoes, then stood and again leaned into me. For a moment I held her against my chest, and at first she sighed, then she groaned as she leaned back. "This is so painful." She kissed me again then reluctantly went out to the front room. At the front door I stopped her again. I kissed her neck and she tilted her head to bare more of it to me.

"You're not making this any easier," she said.

"I hope not."

After another long kiss she dropped her chin, then opened the front door and walked out. I followed her to her car. "Call me from the airport."

"Which one?"

"Both of them."

She unlocked her car door and we kissed once more, then she climbed into her car and started it up, while I stood in the driveway, barefoot and bare-chested, my arms folded. She backed out and I waved as she drove away. I went back to bed, holding her pillow to my face. There was still a trace of her perfume. I couldn't believe how quickly loneliness ensued or how hard it fell, pouring in on me as if her departure had collapsed the walls of some great emotional dam. And I couldn't believe how good I felt for being in such pain.

Faye was lugging a bulging gray duffel, the last of her baggage, out to her father's Cadillac when she saw Jayne, her younger sister, leaning against the hallway wall. Her arms were crossed around herself and her head was slightly bowed. Faye saw her raise a hand to wipe a tear from her cheek.

"Oh, Jayne."

Jayne looked up; her eyes were red and puffy and she began to tremble. Faye went over and put her arms around her, and Jayne dropped her head to her sister's shoulder.

"I don't want you to go."

"Oh, Jayne," Faye repeated. Then Faye took her hand and led her into her bedroom. They sat down next to each other on the pleated bedspread, Faye holding her little sister tightly while tears streamed down their cheeks.

"I was doing so well," Faye said. "I thought I might be able to get out of here without drowning everyone." She forced a smile. "Besides, I thought you were glad I'm leaving. You finally get my stereo."

Jayne didn't smile. "I can't believe you're really leaving."

"It sneaked up on us, didn't it."

"I don't know what I'll do without you. You're my best friend."

"And you're mine. We've been through a lot together. What's that song? 'Skinned our hearts and skinned our knees.' " For a moment Faye just held her, then pressed her lips against Jayne's ear. "I love you, Jayne."

"I don't know how I'll get along without you. Especially now."

"What do you mean?" Faye asked.

"Things are just hard now."

Faye leaned back in concern. "What's so hard?"

"School. Friends. Boys. I just can't make things work."

"Of course you can. You've got every-thing going for you. You're a lot smarter than I am. You have more friends." Faye smiled and brushed the hair back from her sister's face. "Not to mention, you're prettier."

"You don't know. I don't have that many friends anymore. I'm not getting good grades. Dad's going to kill me when he finds out I didn't take calculus."

"Who cares about calculus? You have so many other talents. You're so artistic and creative. I would give anything to have your gifts."

Jayne looked up at her. "I don't want you to go, Faye. Why do you have to go so far? Why can't you just stay in-state? You could go to the U. It's a good school."

Faye just kissed her forehead. "I'll be back at Christmas. It's just a few months. And we'll talk every week on the phone. I promise."

For a moment the sisters were silent. Then Faye's face lit up. "I have a secret," she said. Faye got up and shut the door. "You must swear to never tell anyone."

Jayne wiped tears from her face and nodded. It was something they had done a million times in childhood, mutually sworn to oaths of secrecy.

"You need to promise me, Jayne. This is important."

"I promise. You know I can keep a secret."

Faye reached down the front of her shirt and pulled out the ring. The emerald caught the light from the window and glistened. At the sight of it Jayne leaned forward to examine it. "Oh, Faye." She looked back up. "You're engaged!"

Faye shook her head. "Nope."

Jayne looked perplexed. "It's not an engagement ring?"

"Ask me what my last name is."

It took only a moment for Jayne to understand. "You didn't really . . ."

A broad smile stretched across Faye's face. "I did. We did. Yesterday. I didn't sleep at Shandra's last night."

Jayne raised her hand to her mouth, "Oh, my . . ." She was suddenly smiling. "It was Michael, wasn't it?"

At this Faye laughed and playfully hit Jayne on the arm. "Of course it was Michael. We couldn't wait. You think *you're* worried about Dad finding out about calculus . . ."

"I won't say a word. I promise. Dad won't hear it from me."

"No one better hear it from you. You're the only one who knows."

Jayne smiled at this, pleased to be Faye's sole confidante. "So when are you going to tell Mom and Dad?"

"We're not sure yet. Maybe next summer. Then we'll have a real wedding. I want you to be my maid of honor."

"What was it like?"

Faye smiled dreamily. "It was wonderful. We got married in Wendover in this old chapel. It was kind of a dive, but it didn't matter at all."

"Not the wedding, the honeymoon!"

Faye just smiled. "You'll find out someday."

"Was it everything you hoped it would be?"

"Everything but long enough. But it was more than I ever dreamed." She sighed. "I hope you find someone like Michael. I'm so in love, I'm afraid I won't be able to keep my mind on school."

Just then there was a knock on the door

and Faye shoved the ring back down her shirt. The door opened and Dr. Murrow stepped in, glancing between the sisters. He suspected he had walked in on something, but thought little of it. He was not much on small talk with the girls.

"Are you ready, Faye?"

Faye nodded. "Yes."

Just then Abigail, Faye's fifteen-year-old sister, slipped in behind her father and ran to Faye, throwing herself into her and knocking her back on the bed. "I don't want you to go," she cried. At this Faye laughed. "You guys, I'm not dying here. I'll call every Sunday night. And I'll be back in just a few months for Christmas." Abigail had now pressed her head against Faye's breast, and Faye kissed the crown of her head.

"I love you, Abby."

"I love you, Faye."

Faye stood, her arm still wrapped around Abigail but her gaze fixed on Jayne's eyes. She raised a finger to her lips and winked. "You hang in there, sister."

"Time to go, girls," her father said.

"C'mon," Faye said. "Let's do this."

Jayne stood up and put her arm around Faye, and the three sisters descended the stairway as one.

It was a little after one o'clock when Faye called from the airport. I could barely hear her above the din of the airport terminal.

"Hello, lover."

"I can't believe that after last night you're going to leave me," I said.

"Neither can I."

"You really want to go through all this schooling just to add a few letters to your name?"

"I did that by marrying you," she whispered into the receiver.

"Do you think anyone suspects?" I asked.

"No. But on the way to the airport my father came up with a new name for you."

"The mind reels," I said sardonically.

"He calls you my 'chronic boyfriend.' "

I didn't respond and Faye said buoyantly, "It's progress, Michael. He actually acknowledged the boyfriend part."

"Just in time to get him ready for the husband part."

She hesitated, then said, "Michael, I told Jayne that we're *married.*" She spoke the word so low I could only understand it in context.

"You think that was a good idea?"

"Jayne can keep a secret."

I couldn't deny that. Jayne had aided and abetted our courtship from its inception, covering for us on countless occasions. Faye suddenly said, "I've got to go. They've started boarding. Dad's giving me the eye. Bye, my love."

"Call me when you get there. Just so I know you're safe."

"I'll call. I better go now."

"Faye, remember I love you more than anyone or anything in this world."

I had never said anything like this to anyone before. Even though Faye knew how I felt about her, it still caught her off guard. I could tell from her voice that she was crying. "I love you too, Michael. Good-bye." She blew a kiss into the receiver before she hung up.

CHAPTER FOUR
Another Death

I believe that I now understand what it means to be one with another. In Faye's absence I realize that I'm no longer certain where I leave off and where she begins.

MICHAEL KEDDINGTON'S JOURNAL

The emptiness that had abated with Faye's call as quickly returned, filling me with an ache I could only describe as homesickness. I waited around the house for several hours, read, reviewed my fall class schedule, and mentally tracked Faye's flight. She did not call again, though I was not surprised; as I expected her father would hustle her from the plane to the cab. I finally gave up on waiting and went out for a taco. Then I drove to the city cemetery, parked outside its spear fence along Fifth Street, and ate my dinner.

The locust tree–lined street was vacant as usual. Unless it was some dignitary's funeral (or what we have of them in Ogden), no one ever parked along Fifth. There was no sidewalk and the entrance to the cemetery was two blocks away. I parked there because it was near my mother's grave and I didn't mind climbing the fence.

There were occasional gusts of wind, and leaves fell sporadically from above, littering my Datsun's hood beneath an autumn quilt. When I finished eating, I shoved the food wrappers back into the sack and stowed them on the floor on the passenger's side of the car. Then I got out, hopped the fence, and walked the familiar route to my mother's grave.

I sat down on the blue grass to the side of her headstone. It was a small stone, too small, I thought, though it was more than I could afford at the time. I ran my fingers over her name engraved in the rose granite.

Caitlin Keddington
A LOVING MOTHER
AUGUST 1, 1944–OCTOBER 30, 1988

I made it a point to visit my mother's grave every week. I come to the cemetery to talk to her. I suppose there are those who might think it odd, but there were times that I felt something. An intangible warmth as if she was present. The same kind of feeling you get when you know someone else is looking at you, or is in the same room as you, though you cannot see them. If there is an afterlife, and I believe there is, it makes sense to me that my mother would be there. I don't think death changes a person's soul. My mother was always there for me in life. At least until now. Now I had Faye.

I sat there for a while before I said anything, listening to the eastern wind funneled down the canyon, whistling among the trees of the cemetery. Our marriage would please my mother; I believe she loved Faye from the moment she met her. My mother was already dying of ovarian cancer when I first introduced her to Faye. It was less than a week later that we learned that the cancer had spread throughout her lymph system and the oncologist had given her a schedule to die by. Three months, he said. She lasted eight

months, twelve days, and twenty-one
hours. My mother was a survivor.

From the first moment they met, Faye
had treated my mother with deep respect,
as if she instinctively sensed the heartache
and sacrifice life had required of her.
Though my mother said little of our future,
I knew that she hoped we would somehow
end up together.

"We got married," I said softly. "It's like
you used to say, 'someone's got to win the
lottery.' The ceremony wasn't much, but I
promised to be considerate of her. But I'll do
more than that. I'll cherish her every day we
are blessed with. I'll do everything possible
to make her glad that she chose me. I'll never
leave her. I promise you that. I will treat her
the way you should have been treated. I will
make you proud of the son you raised."

Only the wind answered and I looked
around, then rubbed my hand again across
the stone. A sudden warmth enveloped me.
I left the cemetery and drove in to work.

My shift at the Arcadia had been designed to accommodate my school sched-

ule. Though each day was as unique as our residents could make it, the basics of my routine varied little. I would arrive at four, read the floor report, then commence a quick walk-through of the second floor, establishing eye contact with each of the residents. It was important to do this. This was their home, not mine, and they needed to know who was in it.

At four-thirty, we would begin waking the residents for dinner. At five-thirty sharp—a time actually dictated by the state legislature—dinners would begin to emerge from the kitchen and we would help our residents to the dining room. Once they were settled in we would bring the food carts up to those who preferred to dine in their rooms. When the mealtime was completed we began to help them to bed. By eight most of the residents were asleep.

With the exception of the melancholy I battled, it was an ordinary night; the usual second-floor cast was assembled: Sharon, Brent, and myself. Halfway through my shift I stopped at the room of Margaret and

Hazel. Margaret had complained that her sheets were "too stiff." I wasn't sure what that meant except that we'd have no peace until someone changed her sheets. Margaret was out. The curtain that hung between the room's two beds had not been drawn and Margaret's roommate, Hazel, gazed intently at me while I changed the sheets. Finally she could hold back no longer. "Come here," she commanded.

I finished patting down the bed then walked to Hazel's bedside.

"Yes, Hazel."

She pointed to her roommate's space. "Look."

My gaze followed the trembling finger. After a moment I asked, "What am I looking for?"

"Are you blind?"

"I don't know what you're pointing at, Hazel."

Her aggravation escalated. "Mar-ga-ret's *lamp*," she said, fiercely enunciating each syllable.

I looked at the small, cloth-shaded bed lamp glowing dully on the stand next to her roommate's bed. A similar lamp was on each nightstand throughout the Arcadia.

"What about it?"

"It's brighter than mine." She glared at me indignantly, no doubt awaiting an apology and a speedy resolution to the crisis.

I walked over to the lamp, switched it off, inspected its bulb, then came back to Hazel's lamp and compared the wattage. "They are both sixty-watt bulbs," I said.

"*Anyone* can see that her lamp is brighter than mine. Anyone but a damn fool."

I gazed silently at her for a moment, then I walked over to the lamp, unplugged it, carried it over to Hazel's nightstand, and replaced Hazel's lamp with Margaret's. When I had finished the exchange I said, "There you are. Have a good night."

A smug, satisfied grin rested on Hazel's face. "We'll see how she likes them onions," she muttered triumphantly as I walked from the room.

Around eleven, Sharon brought two cups of coffee to the nurses' station. Next to Helen, Sharon was my best friend at the

Arcadia. Sharon was one of the few employees who had known me before my trial. I had come to classify my life, at least my work life, by that event: B.C. and A.D.—before charged and after dismissal.

In a way, the case made me notorious at the facility, with staff and residents alike, and there were several employees who worked the first-floor day shift who I sensed were afraid of me, as if some part of them still wondered. I believe it's human nature to assume someone is guilty until proven innocent.

"You take cream?" Sharon asked.

"Right. Thanks."

As I brought the cup to my lips, Sharon sat down next to me. "You're quiet tonight."

I sipped my coffee then set the cup down. "Faye left today."

"No wonder." She frowned sympathetically. "When will you see her again?"

"Not until Christmas. Maybe Thanksgiving."

"I'm sorry," she said. One corner of her mouth rose in stifled amusement. "What was Hazel's problem?"

"It was her lamp."

"Broken?"

"No. She didn't think her lamp was as bright as Margaret's."

Sharon smiled knowingly. "Hazel's a masterpiece," she said, and I suspect she meant that more as a Dalí than a Rembrandt. She took a sip of her coffee, then her demeanor fell serious again. "I think we might lose Ruby tonight."

"Have you called her family?"

"I tried. We only have her daughter's number. I've called three times already but no one's home. I just keep leaving messages." She glanced up at a wall clock. "It's been about a half hour. I'll try again."

I downed the coffee. "I'm going back to rounds. Have you seen Brent?"

She laughed cynically. It was the most common question of our shift. Sharon once had a bumper sticker made that read, WHERE'S BRENT?

"What kind of question is that?"

"A dumb one. Do you need help with Ruby?"

"Maybe in a little while."

"I'll get the rest of the residents on the east hallway, then I'll check in on you."

In one of her darker moments, Esther had once told me that nursing homes should be named after western towns, like Last Stop or Death Valley. Despite our culture's fascination with death, we go to great lengths to conceal it from ourselves, pushing it out the back doors of hospitals in unmarked vans, and into secluded corners where we can safely get on with the business of ignoring our own mortality. Corners like the Arcadia. I had witnessed more than a dozen deaths in the time I had worked here. In some ways death was as much a part of my job as was life. Perhaps it's my mother's influence, but I do not believe they are opposites, death and life, just different points on the same continuum.

Ruby had been dying for some time. She was in her late seventies, though she looked much older than that, her body ravaged by the late-onset diabetes that had left her blind. She was crying for her daughter, Rena, when I entered her room. Sharon was seated at her side, holding her hand. The woman's eyes and forehead were covered with a damp cloth for fever. There were also cloths around her neck and under her arms. Her face was chalky pale and her hands and wrists were mottled and purple. She had an IV needle taped to one arm. The incandescent wall lamp above her bed was on and its hood had been turned away, casting long shadows against the room's far wall. On the table next to the bed was a plastic moon-shaped basin and a syringe lying flat next to brown bottles of morphine and Valium.

"What do you need?"

Sharon did not look up. "She wants her daughter."

Ruby's cries were as mournful as anything I had ever heard. "What's the number? I'll call her again."

"I just tried," Sharon said. "I got the answering machine again. Her daughter must be out for the night."

"Or on vacation," I said.

Sharon frowned. "She had her last morphine ten minutes ago. I just gave her some Valium to help calm her."

I looked on helplessly as Ruby's cries rose in volume. Sharon rubbed her hand. "It's okay, Ruby. We're with you."

With the noise rising I went to close her door, when I noticed a woman standing in its threshold. She was slightly older than me, maybe twenty-five, with full, sharp lips and blonde hair that fell to her shoulders. She had fair skin and emerald eyes, too green to be natural, I thought. She stood silently for a moment, hesitantly looking in at the woman, then she walked past me into the room.

"Rena," the old woman again cried out, her voice slurred with the fresh morphine Sharon had administered.

The woman took her hand. "I'm here."

Ruby let out a faint gasp. "Rena," she cried gratefully. "Oh, Rena." Ruby clenched the woman's hand, then raised it, alternately kissing the hand then pressing it against her tear-stained cheek.

The woman crouched down next to the bed while Ruby continued rubbing her hand. In stark contrast to a few moments earlier, the room was silent except for the old woman's occasional muttering and belabored breathing. The young woman lovingly ran her hand through Ruby's hair to comfort her.

I believed it was an incredible coincidence that her daughter showed up when she did. I knew from experience that Ruby didn't have much time left.

"She's just had a heavy dose of morphine," Sharon said to the young woman. "Three milligrams."

"How much longer do you think she has?"

"Not much," Sharon said gently. "I'm sorry." Sharon rose. "We'll leave you alone. If you need anything, just push the call button."

The young woman said nothing as Sharon stepped to my side, putting a hand on my arm to take me out with her. As we left, the woman sat on the chair and lay her head next to Ruby. Ruby touched her head, crumpled the blonde hair between her trembling fingers.

Less than two hours later the young woman walked from the room. Her face was solemn and streaked with tears.

"She's gone," she said softly.

"I'm sorry," I said. I found Sharon and we went to the room, leaving the young woman alone in the hallway. About fifteen minutes later, when Sharon and I emerged from Ruby's room, she was gone.

"Where's her daughter?"

I glanced around. "She was right here. Maybe she's in the bathroom."

We waited a few more minutes, then Sharon checked the restroom door and found it unlocked and the room empty. We walked the second floor, then Sharon went downstairs while I checked the third, but we could not find her daughter anywhere. We met back outside the room. Sharon shrugged in bewilderment. "I guess she had to go."

CHAPTER FIVE
Blythe

It is possible to learn more about compassion in one quiet act of selflessness than in a hundred fiery sermons.

MICHAEL KEDDINGTON'S JOURNAL

As soon as the coroner arrived I left Sharon and went back to my rounds. I had noticed in the daily report that a new resident had been moved into the private room where Della had been. Christopher Thomas Lunt. I had read his file. He was eighty-six, a victim of a stroke that had left him incoherent and the entire left side of his body paralyzed. I had not seen him yet, though Brent had checked on him earlier and brought him dinner.

The door to his room was closed. As I opened it I could hear the soothing inflections of a woman's voice as she read aloud. The room was illuminated only by the small lamp next to the man's bed. To my surprise, sitting on the far side of the bed was Ruby's daughter. She held the old man's hand as she read to him from a paperback book, Anne Rice's *Interview with the Vampire*. She glanced up at my entrance, the green of her eyes visible even in the room's dim lighting. I walked to the side of the bed to take the man's blood pressure.

She lowered the book. "Do you need me to leave?" she asked.

"No. I just need to check his vitals." I adjusted the cuff on his arm. "We've been looking for you."

"Why?"

I thought it an odd question.

"We had some questions about your mother's interment. She also has some personal effects we thought you might want to take with you."

At first she looked at me with a puzzled expression, then said, "Oh, the woman. She's not my mother."

"What do you mean?"

"I've never seen her before tonight. I only came by to ask you something."

"But she knew your name."

She shook her head. "No, she didn't."

"But you said . . ."

"I said that I was there for her. Her eyes were covered. She didn't really know who I was."

I stared at her in disbelief. "Then why did you stay with her?"

She looked at me and her slim, arched brows drew downward. I could not tell if she was perplexed by my question or disappointed that its answer eluded me. "Because she needed someone."

I let her words sink in. I looked at the old man whose hand she now held. "Do you know *him*?"

Her face suddenly lit with childlike merriment. "Oh, yes. He's my grandfather."

I could not help but smile as well. I held his pulse as I counted down seconds on my watch. Then I recorded his stats on a clipboard near his bed. "One-eighteen over seventy-two. That's not bad." I rolled up the cuff. "It would be better if he didn't need to be here."

"That would be better," she agreed.

I started to turn, then stopped. "What was it that you wanted to ask?"

"What?"

"You said you came to Ruby's room to ask us something."

"I wanted to know how late visiting hours run."

"As long as he wants you here."

She smiled. "Thank you."

"Good night," I said.

As I walked out I could hear her start back into the book.

At midnight I went downstairs and clocked out, put my smock in my locker, then stopped in the kitchen and poured myself a cup of orange juice. I tossed the paper cup in the garbage on the way out to my car.

As I wheeled my Datsun around in the parking lot I saw the young woman we had mistaken for Ruby's granddaughter. She was standing by the side of the canyon road just outside the entryway. She was difficult to see in the dark as she wore an indigo sweater and black slacks. I stopped my car next to her. I reached over and rolled down the passenger-side window. "Need a lift?"

She stooped over to look into my car. "Thank you, but no. The bus should be here in a few minutes."

"Where are you headed?"

"Around Twelfth Avenue. The bus goes that way."

"So do I. Hop in."

She hesitated.

"I'm safe. Really."

"All the serial killers say that."

I grinned. "If you're taking the bus you risk your life either way."

An amused smile pursed her lips. She looked inside my car at the mess that had accumulated on the passenger's seat. "Where would I sit?"

"I'll make a place for you." I leaned over, gathered the rat's nest of paper sacks and depleted soft-drink cups and transferred them all to the backseat. She climbed into my car, pulling her sweater in around her.

"Sorry about the mess. I've been living in my car lately." I pulled out onto the canyon road.

"I just appreciate the ride."

"I didn't know the bus ran this late."

"It's from the ski resort. It's the last one of the night."

"Do you always take the bus everywhere?"

"Just today. My car's in the shop." She suddenly turned toward me and extended her hand. "My name's Blythe."

I took her hand. "Blythe?"

"I know, it's not very common."

"I'm Michael. We're a dime a dozen."

I turned back to the road.

"Where do you live?" I asked.

"On Gramercy Avenue. It's about ninth east, a half block off Twelfth. Just east of Monroe."

"It's practically in my backyard." We drove a few blocks in silence. I glanced over at her. "What you did tonight was beautiful." She didn't respond, not verbally at least, and I guessed her silence came from the awkwardness some people feel when complimented. "Your grandfather's new at the Arcadia."

"He was just admitted today. He had a stroke about two months ago. He was in the hospital for a while. When they released him we tried to take care of him at home, but it was too much for us."

"Us?"

"My mother and me." She looked back down. "Really, just me."

"Were you close to him?"

"Very close. He raised me, mostly. My mother checks in and out of our lives."

"Why is that?"

"She's an alcoholic."

I nodded knowingly.

Her voice became more introspective. "I don't know how much longer he has. The doctors say it's not uncommon to have a second stroke. The stroke has already taken most of him from me." She looked out her window. "Sometimes I think he's still all there, just trapped inside a shell that won't let him out." She turned back toward me. "Does it seem strange to you to read to someone who can't respond?"

"I think it's strange that you read Anne Rice to him."

She smiled. "My grandfather loved horror stories."

"We had a resident come out of a coma

after two weeks. He knew everything that had gone on around him."

"How long have you worked at the Arcadia?"

"I started about a year ago. But I took an unplanned leave of absence."

"You're not the guy who was put in jail for killing one of the residents," she asked flippantly.

I looked over at her. "That's me."

She was embarrassed to have blurted it out. She blushed. "I'm sorry. I don't know where that came from."

"I didn't do it."

"I read that they caught the person responsible."

"They did."

"What happened to him?"

"Her. She got a real nasty slap on the wrists. Her father had connections. She was put on probation and fined. I spent more time in jail than she did."

"That's how it is with the rich," she said.

"Yes, that's how it is with the rich," I echoed. "Do you work?"

"Like a slave. I work at the bakery in the

Smith's Food Mart on Washington." She suddenly pointed. "You can turn up there, by the credit union."

"Before I let you off, do you have any painful memories I could remind you of?"

"I'm sorry," she said penitently. Then she said with a pleasant smile, "So you might be a killer after all."

"Maybe."

I turned off Twelfth Avenue. "Now where?"

She pointed toward a small paneled home lit by a porch light. "It's the house with the willow."

I pulled into the driveway. She opened the door and stepped out, then leaned back in.

"You really shouldn't make it a habit to pick up strangers. How do you know it's not me who's the killer?"

"Too late for that. I saw your soul tonight."

CHAPTER SIX
Johns Hopkins

With all my heart I miss Faye. It may be better to have loved and lost than never to have loved at all, but my aching heart is not convinced of it. The teetotaler is grateful to never know the agony of a drink's beckoning.

MICHAEL KEDDINGTON'S JOURNAL

Pine is a verb that is seldom used by my generation, yet it is the word that best described my feelings at that time. I pined for Faye. I dreamt of her. I woke in the morning thinking of her. In my solitary moments I reviewed the mental tapes of our last day and night together, the memory bringing a subtle smile to my lips and the dull ache of separation to my chest.

Faye and I had talked on the phone every night since her departure, though due to our schedules, the first two nights were little more than good-night kisses. I anticipated her evening call as the addict anticipates a fix, knowing all the while that just minutes after she hung up, the rush would wear off and the need for her would be all the greater.

It did not help that I was so alone. Unlike Faye, I did not have many close friends. It was the way my life had always been. I was the quiet one at school, the guy with thrift shop clothes who worked on the lunch line and missed the last hour of school on work release to help support our small family. Though I wanted to, I never played football or any team sport. Those things were a luxury beyond my reach. I imagine that if I were to turn up at a high school reunion I would be met with blank stares and a chorus of "I'm sorry, I don't remember you."

Faye was my best friend and, since my mother's death, my only confidante. My only family. I felt like my heart had moved to Baltimore and I was ready to follow. Tuesday afternoon, a half hour before work, she called me at home.

"You were exhausted last night," I said.

"I was. We had an all-day student orientation."

"How'd it go?"

"It was good, but I'm overwhelmed. Everyone here is brilliant."

"You're in a school of overachievers. Including yourself. How are your roommates?"

"My roommates are . . . interesting."

"That doesn't sound good."

"They're just different. Only one of them is American and she's the least friendly. She's from Cheyenne. One of the instructors told me that she scored the highest MCAT in Wyoming this year. He said she has a photographic memory. She's only going to Johns Hopkins because she got in an argument with the dean of student affairs at Harvard. I told her that you were from Cheyenne and she said, 'Honey, Cheyenne's a big piece o' real 'state. We done got us a McDonald's.' "

"What about the others?"

"Angel and Marci. They're both Chinese. They only speak to each other in Mandarin. Angel's from Taiwan and Marci's from mainland China. I think that causes some tension between them."

"I would think so."

"In a couple of minutes we're all going out for pizza. We thought it would be good to get to know each other better before class starts in the morning."

"Sounds like something you'd arrange."

"Always the social chair."

"Or diplomat. What time is your first class?"

"Seven. Biochemistry. Then I have Cells and Tissues. How about you? Did you get registered for school?"

"I went in to register yesterday. I didn't get all the classes I wanted, but I still had some general ed I needed to pick up, so it's okay. I added a music appreciation class."

"Who's your instructor?"

"MacGregor."

"I had him. He's older than Bach. Lot of good it did me. I still can't tell my Handel from my Haydn. Are you glad to be going to Weber?"

"I think so. Especially after what the U pulled."

"They'll be sorry someday that you're not an alumnus."

"I still may be. They have a good law school."

"So what are you going to do without me around to take up all your time?"

"Suffer mostly. That and work."

She laughed.

"I work every night this week until midnight."

"That's a drag."

"Not really. After our wanton summer of play I can use the money. I just about have my mother's funeral paid off. Besides, work helps me keep my mind off how much I miss you."

She was suddenly quiet. "Do you think being apart hurts more now that we're married?"

"IIow could it not?"

"Does it make you wish that we had waited?"

The tone of her question surprised me. "No. Some pain is worth having."

There was suddenly a loud voice in the background. Faye sighed. "That's Lou Dean. They're waiting for me. I love you, Michael."

"Wait," I said. "Do you wish we had waited?"

She sensed my insecurity. "No," she said reassuringly. "I didn't mean anything by that. I'm lucky to have so much to miss."

"Have fun tonight," I said. "Be safe."

I reluctantly hung up the phone. We were both unaware that Faye was about to meet the woman who would change both of our lives.

CHAPTER SEVEN
Canelli's

I have learned that simple acts of kindness may have profound consequences, though more likely for the giver than the recipient.

MICHAEL KEDDINGTON'S JOURNAL

Canelli's Pizzeria was a student hangout four blocks south of Johns Hopkins Medical Center. It was a mainstay of the campus community and had been around longer than even most of the faculty could recall. It was located below street level, in the basement of a pharmacy, requiring the descent of concrete stairs to enter.

The inside of the restaurant was dark, lit by neon beer signs and bare incandescent bulbs that hung from conduits from an exposed black ceiling crossed with ductwork. The interior walls were brick, though the restaurant's management encouraged personal expression via graffiti and the walls had been scrawled on in paint or ink over and over again in their thirty-plus years of business.

Along one wall were booths with brown Naugahyde benches. The rest of the room was taken up by small square tables covered in black, textured vinyl and adorned with wine-bottles-turned-candle-holders, each one covered over with the multicolored cascade of a thousand candles.

The walls were decorated with framed posters of rock bands, an evolutionary ride through rockdom: Oingo Boingo, Supertramp, the Grateful Dead, the Beatles, the Knack, and a Bob Dylan concert poster. Near the entrance was a cork board layered with the restaurant's own diner reviews, mostly outdated university handbills, and want ads and personals.

There was a pool table, though due to the narrowness of the room, it was situated too close to one wall (the one with the Beatles poster), making it difficult to make some shots. The students had coined the phrase Ringo shot, and among regulars the wall had become part of the strategy of the game.

The menu was Italian-American: pizza, calzone, salads, and pasta. The food was mediocre, but cheap, and it drew a regular clientele of students and other locals, enough to keep the doors open. Canelli's was usually quiet except on weekends, when students crowded the restaurant to unwind, and the beer and music flowed.

A few moments after Faye and her roommates were seated, a woman approached their table, bearing a stack of menus. She was barely five feet in stature, fine-boned, as thin as a Fifth Avenue store mannequin. She had deep brown eyes and mahogany hair that revealed a few grays—though she was young and these were from the mileage of her life, not the years. She wore a name tag that read *Judy.* As she distributed the menus she asked with a faint hint of a Southern drawl, "What may I get y'all to drink?"

Lou Dean sat back in her chair. "What light beers do y'all have?"

The waitress ignored the mockery. "Coors, Miller, and Bud."

"Coors'll be just fine, darlin'."

Faye said, "Just some coffee, please."

"I will have coffee," Angel said.

The waitress looked at Marci.

"A Coca-Cola, please."

". . . and an order of them there cheese pull-a-parts," Lou Dean said.

The waitress scribbled the addition. "I'll be right back with your drinks."

With the waitress gone, Lou Dean eyed the two Asian women, her eyes darting back and forth between them. The two looked alike—even to other Asians. They were both the same height and build and their faces were similar, though Angel was more fair-skinned and slightly broader of face.

"So, Angel, you're from Taiwan."

"I am Marci," she said.

"I am Angel," the other said. "I am from the southern part of Taiwan. The city of Kaohsiung. It is the shipping district," she said, carefully enunciating each word. Both Asian women spoke without the benefit of contractions.

"Didn't ask for a travel guide, sweetie," Lou Dean drawled. "What about you, Marci?"

"I am from Beijing."

"Are you a communist?"

The question appeared to frighten her. Lou Dean enjoyed the reaction.

"Does coming from Cheyenne make you a cowgirl?" Faye asked dryly.

Lou Dean glanced coolly at Faye. "As a matter of fact it does."

A moment later the waitress emerged from a pair of swinging doors, balancing the tray of drinks with one hand. As she neared the women's table she suddenly stumbled, her hand fell, and she dropped the tray. The glass mugs and cups shattered on the tile floor, their beverages surfing around and beneath the table. The women lifted their feet. The entire restaurant paused, then as quickly erupted in cheers and hoots.

The waitress flushed. "I'm so sorry." She took a rag from her apron and crouched down and began to lift the glass shards onto her tray. A man at a neighboring table said, "She dropped a tray the last time I was in here."

The night manager, a stocky, mustachioed man wearing a crimson apron soiled with flour, emerged from the kitchen like an angry bee from its hive. He towered over the woman still crouched to the floor. "Damn, not again! Get a mop," he said tersely. "Hurry."

She looked up anxiously, then hurried off to the kitchen. The manager looked at the women and shook his head. "I'm sorry, ladies. Come over to this table."

The women lifted their things and carried them over. The waitress returned with a mop, while the manager went back for a new tray of drinks. When the waitress had finished cleaning the floor, she returned with a pad, ready to resume where she had left off, though she was clearly humiliated and glanced only furtively at the women.

"What would you like to eat?" she asked, purposely avoiding the *y'all*.

"What don't I mind dropped in my lap?" Lou Dean quipped. "How about a man?"

"I'll have a calzone," Faye said, annoyed at Lou Dean's sarcasm.

The woman scribbled. "Would you like pepperoni or sausage?"

"Pepperoni."

"Make that two," Lou Dean said. The two Asian women stared at the menu.

"I will have piz-za," Marci said, pronouncing the *z*'s.

"What kind would you like?"

"What do you want on your pizza?" Faye asked.

Marci pointed to the ingredients on the menu. "Cheese and piz-za sauce."

"I will have the salad," Angel said. "With ranch dressing."

The waitress said, "I'll be right back." She glanced at Lou Dean. "I'll try not to drop anything on you."

When she was gone Lou Dean turned to Faye. "So, Miss Murrow, tell us about the men in your life."

"What makes you think there is one?"

"I didn't say *one*. With your looks, girlfriend, there are. Tons. Men just love pert little brunettes like you. Besides, you're giddy on the phone every night with someone and I assume it's not Daddy."

"His name's Michael."

"You in love?"

"Yes."

"But he has trouble committing."

"Wrong."

"Good in bed?"

"That's not any of your business."

"Just trying to get to know you a little better. That's why you arranged this little shindig, isn't it? Or maybe there just isn't anything to share. How about it? Has that stained-glass curtain gotten in the way of a little fun?"

"I have fun," Faye said.

"Sure you do. Bingo night at St. Vincent's." She turned away from Faye. "How about you gals. Either of you got men?"

Marci said, "I am married."

A wry smile lit Lou Dean's face. "Really. You look like you're seventeen. And where is the mister?"

"He is in China. With our baby."

"So you're a mother too?"

Marci nodded. "Yes."

Faye fidgeted nervously, rethinking the wisdom of the gathering. She was glad when the waitress returned with their food. The conversation lulled as they ate.

When they finished eating, Lou Dean tallied the bill and wrote down what each owed.

"I'll get the tip," Faye said.

Lou Dean said, "Be my guest."

Faye dropped a ten-dollar bill on the table.

Lou Dean looked at Faye wryly. "That for the floor show?"

"She looks like she could use it."

"She does that."

As they walked away, the waitress walked over to the table and lifted the tip, then glanced over at Faye as she walked out the door.

CHAPTER EIGHT
Jayne

Jayne and I had a long talk today about life. In her voice I recognized the insecurity and self-rejection of my own teenage years. Nowhere is our vision more distorted than when we turn it on ourselves.

MICHAEL KEDDINGTON'S JOURNAL

It was around six o'clock on a Wednesday night that Mrs. Murrow called. It was dinnertime at the Arcadia and Brent and I were on the first floor helping feed the residents. The page said that I had a phone call, and though Faye knew better than to call at dinnertime, I assumed it was her.

"Hello, gorgeous."

There was a long pause. "Hello, Michael, this is Ginny Murrow."

I laughed in embarrassment. "I'm sorry, Mrs. Murrow. I thought you were Faye."

"I'm sorry to call you at work."

"It's okay. How are you?"

"I'm fine," she said politely. "I've been trying to reach you at home, but I can't seem to catch you there."

"Between school and work I'm gone a lot. What can I do for you?"

"Have I called at an inconvenient time?" Her voice was thin and anxious and it suddenly occurred to me that she might have found out about Faye and me. Why else would she call? I felt sick to my stomach.

"No, I can talk."

She again hesitated. "You and Jayne get along quite well, don't you?"

"Sure we do." Jayne was the weak link.

"She talks about you a lot."

I bet she does, I thought. "Jayne's a great girl," I said.

Mrs. Murrow was suddenly quiet. I waited for the hammer to drop.

"We're worried about her."

It took me a moment to comprehend the direction of her statement. "Worried about Jayne?"

"Yes."

I exhaled in relief. "What are you worried about?"

"She's been acting peculiar."

"In what way?"

"A lot of different ways. The truth is we're afraid she's using drugs."

"Why? Did you find some?"

"No. I searched her room while she was away at school, but I didn't find anything."

"Are her friends using drugs?"

"I don't know. She doesn't go out with her friends anymore. She just stays in her room and listens to rock music or plays her guitar."

"Have you talked with her about it?"

"Ben and I tried." She hesitated then added, "Ben lost his temper with her and now she's not speaking to us."

"Maybe Faye should speak with her."

"We would prefer that Faye doesn't know about this. She has enough on her plate. I'm a little concerned that Jayne's behavior might have something to do with Faye leaving. It started about the same time." She paused. "I . . . We were wondering if you would talk to her. We think she might open up to you."

I was surprised by the request. I surmised that they must have exhausted all other recourse. "I can come by this Sunday morning. Will she be there?"

"Oh, you can count on that. Thank you, Michael. We'll see you then."

It was a crisp autumn morning when I drove the Datsun up the crescent driveway of the Murrow home. Abigail was riding her ten-speed in the street and rode back to the house when she saw my car. We talked awhile, then she invited me in and ran to get her mother. Mrs. Murrow came out of the kitchen to greet me. She was wearing a light pastel dress with a string of large pearls; she was prepared to leave for Sunday brunch with the doctor. She always looked young and fresh, I thought, though the rings under her eyes were visible beneath her makeup. Dr. Murrow was in his den just off the foyer. I could see his loafers resting on an ottoman from where I stood, but he never bothered to come out or acknowledge my entrance.

She quietly, succinctly thanked me for coming, then called for Jayne and left me there alone with Dr. Murrow's feet. I suspected she was anxious that Jayne might think she had something to do with my coming over.

Less than a minute passed before Jayne appeared above me at the second-floor railing. Her hair was uncombed. She was barefoot and wore red gym shorts and a black Metallica T-shirt that was wrinkled, as if it had been wadded up then reworn.

I had not seen her for five or six weeks and seeing her brought a smile. I remembered how much I loved her. "What'sup, girl?"

"Hey. What are you doing here?"

"Came to see if you wanted to get a Coke or something."

"Really?" She smiled. "Sure. I was just listening to the Cure. Let me get my shoes."

We drove to a drive-in about six miles from their home. We stayed in my car and had hamburgers, fries, and flavored colas set on a tray clipped to my door's window. Jayne was the only person I've ever known who thought my car was cool.

"Have you heard from Faye?" I asked.

"She called last Sunday. It's a Sunday thing. She'll call again tonight."

"What did she have to say?"

"Not much. At least not to me. My dad pretty much monopolized her. She didn't seem that interested in talking with me."

"She talks about you all the time. She probably just acts a little different because she's overwhelmed with school. How's school going for you?"

The question made her uncomfortable. She shrugged. "You know. It's school."

I changed the topic to something less touchy. "Seen any good movies lately?"

"I haven't seen many movies lately." The conversation lagged. She suddenly asked, "So what's it like being married to someone you can't be with?"

I had almost forgotten that she knew. "It's hard."

"I think it sucks. I think Faye should come home. We'd all be happier."

"We'd be happier, but it would be at her expense. She needs to have this experience."

"I still think it sucks." She put her mouth on her straw, then looked back up to me. Her voice was suddenly heavy. "Will you give me an honest answer if I ask you something?"

"I'll always be honest with you."

"Did you come over because my parents asked you to?"

I scratched my forehead, then said frankly, "Your mother called. She was worried about how you've been acting lately." Jayne said nothing, though she seemed pained. I added, "She cares about you."

"She's never cared before," she said angrily. "My parents don't care squat about anyone but themselves and their country club friends."

"They do care about you."

Jayne looked at me indignantly. "How can you defend them? You of all people. They treat you like dirt."

"I know they do. But I didn't come over because your parents asked me to. I came over because you're my little sister. If something's wrong you can tell me."

Jayne looked down and her eyes began to water.

"I know you wish Faye were here, but she's not. So let me be there for you."

Jayne began to cry, a little at first, then the tears fell copiously and I leaned over and held her. We sat in my car and talked for nearly two hours. Though I tried, I could not pinpoint a single event that had caused such feelings of guilt and self-pity. Not that there weren't problems.

She liked a boy, some popular rich kid who took her out for a while, then just stopped calling. She had gotten physically involved with him, and though she had not gone all the way, she had gone further than ever before and she felt ashamed and guilty for it and humiliated that he dropped her so quickly afterward. She believed that everyone knew about it and her friends were talking about her behind her back. She was mixed up, perhaps no more than every teenager trapped in the adolescent house of mirrors, but she seemed more confused than most.

Jayne made me promise that I wouldn't tell anyone about our conversation, including Faye. As hard as that promise was to keep, I decided that I could not break her confidence. When I suggested that maybe she could talk to a school counselor or her priest, she told me that outside of Faye, I was the only adult she really trusted. Still, she promised she'd think about it.

There are people, like Faye, who study better with a Coke in hand, the television on, and the stereo blasting, as if focusing through such clutter sharpens the intellect. After enduring two hours of silence at the school library, Faye decided for a change of venue. She walked four blocks to Canelli's with a backpack of books slung across her shoulder.

She sat down at a table in the corner. It was nearly three, the doldrums between lunch and dinner, and the restaurant was quiet, except for the jukebox. There was only one other couple seated and only one waitress working. The same waitress from Faye's previous visit. Faye still remembered her name. Judy.

Faye glanced at the menu, decided on a meal, then looked around for service. The waitress was standing over an empty booth, apparently talking to herself. It struck Faye as a curious sight and she leaned out from her table. There was a pair of small feet in bright yellow socks sticking horizontally out from the booth. The waitress stooped to pick up a pile of papers that had fallen to the floor. As she set them on the table, a child's head emerged from below the table. She was a small girl with dark eyes and auburn hair that fell several inches past her shoulders.

The waitress suddenly glanced back and Faye raised her hand. The waitress kissed the little girl on the forehead then crossed the room to Faye's table. She rubbed her hands as she walked, as if they were cold.

She was dressed more casually than on Faye's previous visit. She wore an over-sized sweatshirt and baggy denim jeans and her hair was drawn back in a tortoise-shell comb except for a few strands that fell over her face. She smiled when she saw Faye.

"Hi. You're back."

"This place is conducive to studying."

"I've never heard that before. Most don't

think it's conducive to eating." She lifted her pad. "What can I get you?"

"I'll have your mozzarella and tomato salad. What kind of dressing does that come with?"

"A pesto dressing."

"That will be fine. Also a slice of garlic bread and a Diet Coke."

The waitress put the pad in her pocket. "I'll be right back with your drink." She stopped and turned back to Faye. "By the way, thanks for the tip the other night."

"You're welcome. You're probably the first waitress in history to thank a customer for a tip."

"I work just for tips."

Faye studied until the dinner crowd began to arrive, raising the overall noise to a decibel level even her thoughts couldn't penetrate. She had paid her bill an hour earlier, so she just gathered her books and notes into her backpack and left a tip on the table. As she was making her way out she found the aisle blocked by the torso of the waitress's little girl, her body stretching across the tile floor. Faye stooped over her.

"Hi, there."

The child glanced around fearfully, then quickly crawled under the table. Then she climbed up onto the bench. The table was scattered with crayons and a few pieces of paper. The girl put her arms over them, as if to hide what she was doing.

"Hi, there," Faye repeated.

She looked up at Faye warily. "Hi."

"What are you coloring?"

"A monster."

Faye looked at the little girl. She was maybe five, with a broad face and penetrating brown eyes. Faye noticed her bangs were cut at a slight angle. "A monster? May I see it?"

The little girl pushed the paper toward her. There were two amorphous yellow blobs encompassed by a black scribble.

"Those are his eyes," she said as she took back her art. "You shouldn't look at it. It's scary."

"It is," Faye agreed.

"I've seen you. Over there." She pointed

toward the corner of the room that Faye had just left.

"I've seen you too."

"Where is your house?"

"I live by the school down the street. I come here to read."

"Most people come here to eat. My mommy gives them food."

"But you and I come here to read too. I think that's better." She looked at the table. "What do you have there?"

Faye reached over and lifted a reader. *Max and Clax.*

"Is that a good book?"

She nodded. "I can read."

"That's wonderful."

"I'm a big girl."

"You are." Faye sat down on the bench next to her. "My name's Faye. What's your name?"

The little girl watched Faye sit, then resumed her coloring, her hand moving in broad circles over a sheet of typewriter paper. "I can't tell you."

"You can't?"

"My mommy says not to tell anyone."

"Oh. Is it because I'm a stranger?"

"It's 'cause we're playing a game."

"What game are you playing?"

"Hide-and-seek."

Faye smiled amusedly. "Who are you hiding from?"

"Daddy." She pushed a paper toward Faye. "You can color too. You have to use both sides of the paper. Some of the crayons are broke."

Just then the waitress walked up to the booth. "Sarah."

Faye turned. "You have a sweet daughter. She was showing me her drawings."

The waitress looked pensively at Faye, then to her daughter. "Sarah, go wash your hands. It's time to eat."

"Can we go to McDonald's?"

"No."

Faye perceived the woman's discomfort. She rose, lifting her books with her. "Well, I'll be on my way. I'll see you later, Sarah."

"Bye," the child said.

The waitress watched Faye exit, then took the little girl by the hand to the restroom. "What did you talk about with the lady?"

"I told her we were playing hide-and-seek."

The waitress's face stiffened. "We don't tell anyone about our game. Remember?" She crouched down in front of the child until their faces were nearly level. "Don't ever talk to that lady again."

CHAPTER NINE
Weber State

There are times that the most innocent of gestures may lead to wrongdoing. This is nowhere more evident than in matters of the heart.

MICHAEL KEDDINGTON'S JOURNAL

Weber State University was not part of my plans. The previous fall I had been awarded the University of Utah's most prestigious scholarship, the President's Award, but it was taken away before I ever received it—when I was accused of a felony. Despite my innocence, the U never reinstated the scholarship.

The one (and only) benefit to my trial's publicity was that the details of my scholarship had been written up in Ogden's local newspaper as an appendage to the article. After my acquittal, one of the administrators at Weber called to offer me an academic scholarship in case the U did not reinstate mine. I accepted the offer. Even though Weber State is a considerably smaller institution than the University of Utah, as I drove to school each morning I was glad of my decision, as Weber was only eight miles from my home and the U was at least an hour commute each way— meaning I would have had to rise by five to make it to school on time. Considering that I didn't get home from work until twelve-thirty in the morning, it was a blessing.

With the commencement of school, I cut back on my work schedule, dropping my weekend shifts. The only other change in routine was that I didn't see Blythe for a while. I was surprised at this. For more than four weeks Blythe visited her grandfather every night without fail and we had gotten to know each other as I interrupted her nightly visits to take her grandfather's vitals. Once, on one of the slower nights, we stepped out into the hallway and I listened to her talk about her grandfather's condition. The conversation evolved into a disclosure of her tremendous fear of losing him. He was everything to her. Though I did my best to console her, I felt hopelessly inadequate to such a task. He was a lucky man, I thought, whether he knows it or not. There were too many lonely in the Arcadia.

I walked in on a Thursday night to find Blythe back at her grandfather's side reading aloud from Wolfe's *The Bonfire of the Vanities*.

"You've moved up a literary rung."

She lay down the book. "You can only read so many vampire stories and go home alone at night."

I walked to her grandfather's side, adjusted the blood pressure cuff around his forearm, and began pumping air into it. "He's been asking for you."

"He has?"

"In his own way. He's been acting differently. Says your name repeatedly." I released the pressure, watching the needle fall. "Tuesday he kept saying 'real honey, Bee.' "

Blythe looked down with a serene smile at the old man. "When school started a few of the bakery employees quit, so I've been working overtime."

"I thought you were going back to school."

"I did. In fact I saw you there today. Over by the commons."

"You should have waved or something."

"I was on the other side of the grounds. You were walking fast."

"I'm always walking fast. My classes are on opposite ends of the campus."

"What are you taking?"

"My major's English. But I have a minor in philosophy."

She sat up in her chair. "What do you want to be when you grow up?"

"A lawyer. An attorney friend of mine recommended that I pursue an English major."

"Why philosophy?"

"Why does anyone take philosophy? Man's search for meaning."

"Well, if you discover the meaning of life in Weber's philosophy department let me know."

"What do they say about college philosophy? You remember just enough to screw up the rest of your life."

She laughed, then looked down at her grandfather. "Would you like a drink, Granddad?"

He began mumbling incoherently. She brought a glass to his lips, guiding the straw to his mouth with her slender fingers. She turned to me and said, "A friend of mine's throwing a party this Saturday. I was wondering if you'd like to go with me. If you don't have to work." She spoke quickly, as if she were nervous.

The invitation caught me off guard. "I'm sorry. I can't."

She moved the glass from her grandfather, then touched the sides of his mouth with a napkin. "You're working that night?"

"No. It's . . ." To the embarrassment of us both I stumbled on my reply. "It's . . ."

"It's okay," she interjected. "You don't need an excuse."

"It's not that. I have a steady girlfriend."

There was an unmistakable glint of disappointment in her eyes. "I'm sorry. I didn't know." She turned away from me to her grandfather, placing the straw back against his lips. After a moment she said, "May I ask you something?"

"Of course."

"If you weren't already committed to someone, would you have said yes?"

I looked at her then smiled. "Yeah, I would have."

She likewise smiled. "I hoped so. I've really enjoyed your company."

"And I've enjoyed yours." I turned back toward the door. "Well, I better go. Good night."

"Good night," she replied. She lifted her book and turned her attention back to the old man.

CHAPTER TEN
Unexpected News

I do not know why we delude ourselves that life is predictable and safe, when it's really just a carton of eggs—always just one stumble away from being scrambled.

MICHAEL KEDDINGTON'S JOURNAL

Faye stared through the darkness at the asbestos ceiling tiles, feeling the acrobatics of her stomach. She felt cramped as well as nauseous and she hoped that it was her period and not the stomach flu. She could not afford to miss class.

It was still dark, not yet five A.M., ten minutes before she usually woke. She reached over, turned off her alarm, and forced herself up from bed. She sat a moment on its edge, then collected from the floor her texts that she had been reading the night before.

Faye was always the first one up in the dorm, rising forty-five minutes before the rest of the women, to study alone in the kitchen beneath the confined glow of a reading lamp. She lay her books on the kitchen table, sat down, and started to read. Three pages into the text she bolted to the bathroom and vomited. She was leaning over the toilet breathing heavily, her hands supporting herself on her thighs, when Angel looked in on her.

"Are you okay, Faye?"

Faye groaned. "I've got the stomach flu."

Angel went to the sink and soaked a washcloth in hot water. She wrung it out, folded it in half, and handed it to Faye.

Faye wiped her face with it, then held it to her forehead. "Thank you."

"You are welcome," Angel said. "I will make gingerroot tea. It will help your stomach."

"Thank you."

Faye flushed the toilet then went back out to the kitchen to resume her studies.

That evening Lou Dean walked into the kitchen to find Faye seated at the table eating sugared cereal while she read from a biology text. Next to her bowl was a partially eaten tuna sandwich on marble rye.

Lou Dean looked at the food then Faye. "Either you're not sick anymore or you're trying to make yourself sick."

"Tuna and Lucky Charms sounded good for dinner."

Lou Dean cast a sideways glance, then went to the refrigerator and brought out a bagel and a tub of cream cheese. "So I guess we don't need to quarantine you after all."

"Apparently not." Faye took another spoonful of cereal.

Lou Dean spread cream cheese on the bagel then sat down at the table across from Faye. "No aching joints? Fever?"

"What are you, a doctor?"

"Workin' on it," she said.

"It mostly went away by lunchtime."

"Any other symptoms?"

Faye smiled at her inquisitiveness. "Nothing besides the usual PMS. My breasts are a little sore."

"Then you're on your period."

"No. Actually I'm late."

Lou Dean nodded, took another bite of her bagel, then asked casually, "Are you pregnant?"

Faye stopped eating. A distinct look of panic crossed her face, in contrast to the smile of amusement that curled Lou Dean's lips.

"So our good little Catholic girl *does* know how to have fun."

Faye did not finish her meal. She pulled on her coat and rushed five blocks to the nearest drugstore.

It was around nine o'clock mountain time when Faye called. I caught the phone on its second ring. "Arcadia Care Facility."

"Michael?"

Faye's voice was so full of distress that it took me a moment to recognize it. "Faye? Are you okay?" She didn't answer. "What's wrong, Faye?"

Her words came naked. "Michael, I'm pregnant."

I was stunned and, for at least a couple of breaths, speechless. "Are you sure?"

"I took two home pregnancy tests. They were both positive."

"How did that happen?"

"Dumb question, Michael."

"But it was only one night."

"Well, it was enough. You're going to be a father."

The word resounded with incredible potency. *Father.* I took a deep breath. "Have you told your parents?"

"Oh, right," Faye said sarcastically, "I called them first thing. Congratulations, Mom and Dad, your daughter's dropping out of medical school to have a baby." I didn't reply and her voice turned more contrite. "I'm sorry. I'm just upset. What are we going to do?"

"I'll come out. I'll fly out tomorrow."

"I've got school, Michael. There's nothing you can do here anyway."

"I just thought being together would help."

She didn't reply and neither of us spoke for a while. Finally she said, "I've got to go. I'll talk to you tomorrow."

I didn't know what to say but to tell her that I loved her. As I hung up the phone my mind reeled as this new labyrinth unfolded before me.

CHAPTER ELEVEN
Autumn

I feel as if the fuse has been lit on a bomb that I am helpless to disarm.

MICHAEL KEDDINGTON'S JOURNAL

It was as if the road map of our future had blown out the car window. Faye's announcement changed everything. Appropriately, perhaps, even the weather changed. In an unusually early snowfall, the first three days of October, northern Utah got hit by a storm leaving measurable snow in the mountains and Wasatch foothills. The Arcadia got at least fourteen inches, though some of the drifts crested at more than three feet.

Faye and I spoke every day. She determined that she would likely start showing about the time she was coming home. Christmas. Until then there was nothing either of us could do but prepare for the inevitable. If only we knew what that was.

The eleventh of October was my birthday. For the most part it was an uneventful day, serving up the usual weighty portions of school and work. It was a day that I especially missed Faye. She woke me at five-thirty to wish me a happy birthday before she ran off to class. I was pretty tired and fell back to sleep the moment she hung up. About all I remembered of our conversation was that she promised to call back when I was awake.

Helen greeted me on my arrival at work with a large cake with white marzipan frosting, which we cut at dinnertime in the dining room. By the time I was through helping the residents to it, it was gone except for a remnant of the frosting border left on the cardboard square.

Later that evening, at a quarter of ten, Sharon and I were seated next to each other in the nurses' office going over the daily patient reports when Brent stuck his head through the doorway.

"A horse walks into a bar, sits down at the counter, and orders a beer. The bartender brings it over and asks, 'Why the long face?'"

I glanced over at Sharon. As a rule we tried not to encourage Brent. Tonight he was undeterred by our lack of enthusiasm and quickly launched into his next one. "This hamburger walks into a bar. He sits down at the counter and asks the bartender for a drink. The bartender says, 'Sorry, we don't serve food.' "

I smiled painfully. Sharon groaned, shaking her head. The reaction was enough for Brent and he grinned in triumph as he walked out. A few moments later he stuck his head back in.

"Enough pain, Brent," Sharon said.

"No such luck. The Griff has pleasured you two enough for one night. I came to tell Mikey that his girlfriend's here with a surprise."

I didn't bother to look up from the patient's chart I was reading. "My girlfriend's in Baltimore."

"Your other girlfriend. Blondie."

He smiled haughtily as I glanced up. I set the chart aside and walked out to find Blythe standing in the hallway, across from the L-shaped nurses' counter. She was

wearing an ash-colored, formfitting body-
suit with a black sweater. In her arms was a
large cake. She smiled when she saw me.
"Happy birthday. I'd sing for you but I
can't."

I smiled. "How'd you know it was my
birthday?"

"I have my sources."

Sharon's voice came from the back
room. "Leave me out of this, unless you
plan to share the cake."

"Come on back," I said.

Blythe stepped around the counter,
handing me the cake. "It's carrot cake."

"I guessed that from the little frosting
carrots on top."

"It took me twenty minutes to do those
carrots, thank you very much."

"You made this?"

"Of course. That's what I do. I'm a professional." She held out a bright yellow envelope. "And I brought this." I set the cake
down on a table and took the envelope. It
was not sealed, so I untucked its flap and
extracted its card. Blythe's script was fluid
and appealing.

Dear Michael,

I am grateful to you for all you have done for my grandfather and me. You have a good heart (as well as a beautiful face, but I won't go there). I don't think you know how much you have helped me during this difficult time. I always feel at peace when you are around. I hope this is a good birthday for you. I, for one, am glad that you were born! I hope that you will consider me your friend.

Love,

Blythe

P.S. I still wish I had found you first.

"It's kind of sentimental," she said.

I set it aside. "It's nice. Thank you."

"May I give you a hug?"

"Of course," I said. She lifted her arms around me, pressing her head against my shoulder. "I really don't know what I would do without you right now. You're a good man."

Just then Brent walked in. He looked at

us and his eyebrows rose as if he had walked in on something interesting.

"When it rains, it pours," he said. "Telephone, big guy. Line three." Then he mouthed silently, "*It's the other one.*"

I looked at him quizzically. "What?"

His face moved in exaggerated motion, still silent. "The other *one.*"

"The other what?" I asked openly.

He looked at me as if I were stupid. "The other *woman,*" he blurted out.

Blythe winked at me. "I'll step out."

When she was gone Brent said, "Man, you're thick."

Sharon got up and left, again shaking her head. She was always shaking her head or rolling her eyes around Brent. I lifted the phone. "Hi, beautiful."

"Hi, birthday boy."

"How are you feeling today?"

"Blue. We should be together today."

"We should be together every day. How about I pack up and come on out?"

"I wish. Did you get my present?"

I didn't know what she was talking about. "The briefcase?"

"I overnighted you something. It should have arrived this morning."

"That's why. I went straight from school to work today. I'm sure it's at home. Or at one of the neighbors'. Now there's a frightening thought."

"Have you had a nice day?"

"It's been all right. They had a party for me here tonight. You haven't lived until you've had twenty octogenarians sing you happy birthday. By the end it sounded more like a dirge."

Faye laughed.

"Jayne called earlier."

"How was she?" Faye asked.

"She was okay."

"She seemed really distant when I called last Sunday. I worry about her."

I almost said something but thought better of it. "She's a teenager," I said, as if that explained everything.

"What are you doing now?"

"We're just about to eat some carrot cake."

"Oh? Who brought that?"

"A friend."

"Who?" she asked casually.

"Her name is Blythe."

Faye paused, then asked with a guarded voice, "Do I know her?"

"She's someone I met here."

"Then she has varicose veins older than me."

"No, she's our age. Her grandfather's a resident."

"Is she pretty?"

I had never heard Faye like this before. "You're jealous."

"Should I be?"

The question bothered me. "What do you think?" I asked.

"I think we're two thousand miles apart and I'm carrying your baby," she said tersely. She was suddenly quiet, and when she spoke again her voice had fallen. "I'm sorry. That wasn't fair. It's the pregnancy talking."

"I understand," I said gently. "I know it's hard."

"This is killing me, Michael. I have so much work to do. I'm nauseous half the time and tired all the time. I've missed two classes this week. I just found out that I can't take Anatomy."

"Why?"

"Because it requires work on a cadaver and I can't be pregnant and work around formaldehyde. I don't know if I can keep this up."

I raked my hand back through my hair. "I'm sorry," I said, though not really sure what I was apologizing for.

"Me too," she said.

I hung up the phone discouraged. I took a deep breath, then walked out of the back room. Blythe was sitting across from the counter in a chair with a built-in scale for weighing our residents. Hector, one of our more virile ninety-year-olds, was standing a few feet away, ogling her, while she pretended not to notice. I waved her on back.

"I see you made a friend."

"They're always married or part of the geriatric set," she said.

"I'll get some plates."

"I beat you to it." She lifted a thin stack of paper plates and plastic forks. "I got some from the dining room." As we walked back into the room she said, "Brent told me you already had cake tonight."

"Brent talks too much. Helen brought in a cake, but I didn't get any of it. The residents ate it all."

She suppressed a laugh. "That's kind of pathetic."

"It worked out well, actually. It had marzipan frosting. I loathe marzipan." I cut a piece of cake and handed it to Blythe.

"Sitting in that chair out there makes me think I should pass on the cake."

"The scale's five pounds off," I said.

"Off which way?"

"It's heavy," I said.

She reached for the plate. "I'll take that."

She sat down at the table while I sat on the edge of a desk.

"This is good," I said.

"You say that like you're surprised."

"No." Then I said lightly, "Maybe a little."

"Why is that?"

"You don't look like you could cook."

"What does that mean?"

I retreated. "I don't know."

"Whatever you meant, I'll take it as a compliment." As we finished our cake Blythe said, "Is everything okay?"

"Why do you ask?"

"You just seem kind of down."

"It was the phone call."

"Want to talk about it?"

"No," I said simply.

She smiled at my frankness. "I understand. If I can do anything."

"Thanks. And thank you for the cake and the card. It was a nice surprise."

"You're welcome. Happy birthday, Michael." She lifted her empty plate. "Where's the garbage?"

"I'll take it."

"Do you mind if I take a piece of cake to my grandfather?"

"Of course not." I lifted the knife. "Edge or center piece?"

"He likes frosting."

I cut a corner piece and put it on a plate along with a fork. Blythe smiled, and carried the cake down the darkened hallway to her grandfather's room. Brent passed her on the way and stopped and watched her walk. When she was out of sight he said to me in a low voice, "Man, how *do* you do it?"

When I arrived home that night there was a package partially protruding from the mail slot at the side of my door. It had been signed for by a neighbor who had brought it over and left it. Considering my neighborhood, I was amazed that it showed no sign of being tampered with. I brought it inside, sat down on my bed, and peeled back its wrappings. Inside was a jewelry box of cranberry-hued crushed velvet. It contained a plain gold wedding band and a note folded in squares. I slid the ring on, then unfolded the note.

Here's your leash. I love you with all my heart. Happy birthday—Faye.

Two days later, Friday the thirteenth, I was sitting alone in the student union cafeteria when I saw Blythe balancing a salad and a drink on a cafeteria tray as she scouted for a place to sit. It was sleeting outside and the cafeteria was full to capacity with diners as well as refugees from the weather. I called to her but she could not hear me over the din of the cafeteria. I stood up and waved her over. She smiled when she saw me.

"Thanks for saving me a place," she said facetiously. She set her tray on the table.

"Don't mention it."

She sat down across from me, examining the contents of my tray. A doughnut and a slice of banana cream pie. "Is that your lunch?"

"All I really want is sugar," I said.

"You and Andy Warhol. How's your day?"

"A little boring."

"I could stand some boring."

"What's up?"

"My mother's back."

"How often does that happen?"

"Every six months or so. She's pressuring me to sell the house. She's already called two real estate agents who I had to send away."

"Why does she want to move?"

"She doesn't. She just wants the money. It doesn't matter to her where she lives. She lives in her car most of the time anyway."

"Is the house hers to sell?"

"No. It's my grandfather's. But he gave me power of attorney. He knew what he was doing. My mother would have drunk it away years ago. When she found out I have power of attorney she accused me of seducing him."

I was suddenly angry. "Your mother's a sick woman."

"That she is," she said thoughtfully. "I can't wait until she leaves. She usually sticks around for less than two weeks, so I don't expect it will be much longer." She feigned a smile. "But enough of my pathetic life, how was the rest of your birthday?"

"You pretty much saw the high points," I said.

"You looked stressed when I left you."

"I was stressed."

She poked a fork at her salad. "Still don't want to talk about it?"

I think to the surprise of both of us, I said abruptly, "Faye's pregnant."

She glanced up with wide eyes. "Oh, my. You found this out on your birthday?"

"No, we've known for a couple weeks. But it's getting more difficult for her."

Blythe considered the predicament. "Does it mean she'll have to drop out of school?"

"Maybe. I don't think they can make her, but her father can. He's already warned us that if we end up connected in any way he'll cut her off financially. I think pregnant counts as connected."

"I would think so," she said. "So what now? Will you marry her?"

I felt suddenly uncomfortable. "I haven't been completely honest with you. We *are* married. We eloped the day before she left for school. We've been keeping it a secret."

The news of our marriage seemed to affect her even more than that of Faye's pregnancy. "Well, since we're coming clean here, I was married once. Sort of."

"How can you sort of be married?"

"It's possible."

"Tell me about it."

She looked pained by my request. "It's not a very good story. But at least it's short. We were only married for four weeks."

"Four weeks. How does that happen?"

"Like I said, it's not a very good story." She changed the subject. "So, Mr. Keddington, are you ready to be a daddy?"

"No."

She thought about it. "You'll make a good father."

"Why is that?"

"You have a good heart. He'll be handsome at any rate."

"I'll take that as a compliment. And if it's a girl?"

"Then she'll look like her mother. I'm sure that's a good thing."

"Yeah," I said thoughtfully. "That would be a good thing."

Blythe went back to her salad and I could not help but think that she was saddened by our conversation.

CHAPTER TWELVE
Thanksgiving

If variety is the spice of life,
routine is the bread of it.

MICHAEL KEDDINGTON'S JOURNAL

The weeks leading to the holidays were monotonous; a daily rerun of school and work. I had classes every weekday from eight to one, recessed an hour earlier on Fridays. After school I ate lunch, then studied until it was time for work. I worked from four until midnight every night except weekends. On Saturdays I slept in until noon. I used the weekends to heal, catching up on housework, homework, and sleep.

As predictable as each day was, after the turbulent changes of the previous two months I welcomed the routine—even if Faye's pregnancy rendered it all temporary.

My schedule did not leave much time for

a social life, but I didn't really care. My biggest problem was not time, but distance. My social life had moved to Baltimore.

There was one benefit to Faye's absence. With the exception of my escalating phone bill, her absence made it easier to save money. By the first of November I had paid off my mother's funeral and was now caching away a sizable portion of each paycheck.

Faye too had found her own routine, absorbed into the rhythm of med school. Classes and schoolwork took a lot out of her, and though we talked every night, we talked less frequently about her pregnancy. She didn't have the emotional energy to discuss it. The one exception was Faye's call around the middle of November when she had returned from her obstetrician having heard the baby's heartbeat. It was the first time she seemed excited about her pregnancy. Up until then the reality of the baby had been nothing more than morning sickness and a pink tint on a home pregnancy test.

Faye's visits to Canelli's had also become a part of her weekly routine. Judy, the waitress, was always there, along with her daughter, though the little girl now hid or would cover her eyes whenever Faye would look her way. Faye wondered at the child's new behavior and guessed that her mother had learned what had been revealed about the game of hide-and-seek from Daddy. Perhaps it was the prospect of her own approaching motherhood that drew her to the child. Whatever the reason, despite the burden of school, Faye could not free her mind of the little girl.

The night before Thanksgiving break Faye went to Canelli's alone. With the impending holiday the restaurant was mostly quiet and Faye stayed longer than usual, studying until midnight, nursing a steady stream of Diet Cokes.

After a two-hour stretch of reading she took her eyes from the text and stretched her neck. Three booths down from her the little girl was asleep on a bench with a blanket around her. Faye drained the rest

of a Coke then glanced around for the waitress. She was in the drink station near the
opposite end of the restaurant. Standing
next to her was the night manager, the curt
little mustached man who had mercilessly
berated her the night she'd dropped the
drinks. Faye could see that his hand rested
on the taut curve of her waist, then
watched as it slid down to her hip. At first
Faye wondered if they might be lovers,
then she saw the waitress turn from him.
Her eyes were dark and angry. The man
seemed undisturbed by her reaction, even
slightly amused. She said something in-
audible and walked away from him,
though his eyes did not leave her. Faye
raised her hand and the waitress walked
over to her table. Characteristically, she
was rubbing her hands.

"Ready for another Coke?"

"That and my check." Faye started to
speak, then caught herself. The waitress
paused. "Anything else?"

"You don't have to put up with that."

The waitress looked at her with a blank
expression. "With what?"

"I saw what he did. How he touched you."

A look of uneasiness fell over the waitress. "It's not a big deal," she said, the sentiment betrayed by the pain in her voice.

"It is a big deal, and you don't have to put up with it. One call to the . . ."

The waitress interrupted. "Thank you, but I can handle it."

"Maybe you think it's none of my business, but jerks like that need to be reported."

She looked at Faye and said sharply, "I don't need to be told what I need to do. I know all too well."

She abruptly turned and walked back to the kitchen, leaving Faye nonplussed by her reaction. A moment later she returned with Faye's drink. Without a word she deposited the drink on the table, avoiding Faye's gaze. There was unmistakable tension.

"I didn't mean to upset you," Faye said.

The woman glanced at her. Her face was tight and wan. "Will that be everything for tonight?"

"Yes."

She dropped the check on the table. "Thank you for coming in."

The day before Thanksgiving break, Jayne sat in her fourth-period chemistry class, her shoulders slack, doodling on a piece of lined paper to the undercurrent of her teacher's drone. When the bell rang she shoved her books in her backpack. As she stood her teacher said, "Miss Murrow, I would like a word with you." He walked over to his desk in the front corner of the class and sat.

A few students glanced over sympathetically. Jayne sat back down at her own desk, waiting for the students to leave. When the room was empty except for the two of them, Jayne sauntered up to his desk. Her teacher looked up at her and she averted her gaze, avoiding his eyes. "I've got to get to my next class," she said sullenly.

"I'll give you a note," he replied. "I want to know what's going on."

"With what?"

"With you. Is it that you don't understand

the work? Are there problems at home? Help me here."

"Everything's fine."

"Except your grade." He motioned to a chair next to his desk. "Here, sit down." Jayne remained standing. He gazed at her, then chose to ignore her insolence.

"I finished grading tests last night. You failed your exam."

Jayne flinched, but said nothing.

"You haven't turned in your homework for two weeks. If you're going to pass this class you're going to have to make some changes. Now I don't usually do this, but since you've been an exemplary student in the past I'm willing to accept your homework late. But I'll need it before the end of the quarter."

Jayne swallowed, but still did not speak. The teacher's voice softened.

"Jayne, what's wrong? You were one of my best students last year. What's changed?"

Students from the next period began to wander in and Jayne looked around, then toward the wall, fighting back the tears that welled up in her eyes. "Everything," she said. "Everything's changed." She quickly turned and ran out the door.

Less than half the students at Johns Hopkins Medical go home for the Thanksgiving holiday, and the majority of those live in the surrounding cities or states. It was simply too short a break to make travel worthwhile. Faye did not come home for Thanksgiving, but spent the day with some of her parents' friends, at the home of a former colleague of Dr. Murrow's who was now the chief cardiologist at the National Heart, Lung, and Blood Institute in Bethesda.

Faye and I had discussed my flying out for Thanksgiving but, in the end, decided against it. It would have meant my having to work Christmas week. As part of a barter, I had arranged to work Thanksgiving Day in exchange for other days off. I had become proficient at such haggling, trading days and shifts with the savvy of a Wall Street broker—one Thanksgiving Day shift and a Christmas Eve double for a

Christmas Day and one future first-round draft pick.

It actually wasn't bad working Thanksgiving if you had no other plans. More than half the residents had been picked up by family, leaving the home quieter than usual. The kitchen prepared a Thanksgiving dinner for those left behind. Nothing to adorn the cover of *Family Circle*, but a cut above the usual fare. Pressed turkey roll (or pureed turkey), mashed potatoes and creamed corn, turkey gravy, stuffing, cranberry sauce, rolls, and butterscotch pudding for dessert.

Sharon and Brent were both off and a newly hired nurse from the first floor was assigned to assist me. It was one of the few days all year that I found time during my shift to study—something I was truly thankful for as the end of autumn quarter was only a week away and finals loomed.

More significant, Faye's return was only a few weeks away.

CHAPTER THIRTEEN
The Gift

I have come to believe that we do not walk alone in this life. There are others, fellow sojourners, whose journeys are interwoven with ours in seemingly random patterns, yet, in the end, have been carefully placed to reveal a remarkable tapestry. I believe God is the weaver at that loom.

MICHAEL KEDDINGTON'S JOURNAL

Faye's last day at school before Christmas break was the twenty-second. In his eagerness to get his daughter home, Dr. Murrow directed his secretary to schedule Faye's flight out as early as possible. She followed his instructions to the letter, scheduling a six A.M. flight out of Baltimore, neglecting the fact that Faye still had classes that day. By the time her error was discovered, the flights out of Baltimore were overbooked with holiday traffic. To everyone's dismay, Faye could not get a confirmed seat home until the afternoon of the twenty-third.

With the conclusion of class there was a mass exodus, leaving the campus nearly deserted for those left behind, the majority of whom were students from foreign countries. Lou Dean had a cab waiting for her ten minutes after class and sped off to Baltimore-Washington International Airport without saying good-bye to anyone. Angel and Marci went to a movie; the holiday meant nothing to them but a break from class.

Faye ate dinner alone at the Green House cafeteria, then, beneath the fall of a light snow, started back to her dorm for a quiet night of reading. Reading had always been one of Faye's favorite pastimes, and she had not read for pleasure since the beginning of school. The street was still, except for an occasional car passing along the slushy streets and the muffled laughter coming from the restaurants along Charles Street. She had never felt so homesick as she did at that moment, and melancholy set in like an influenza with all its attendant aches and pains.

It was then that Faye had a peculiar thought. She had learned at an early age that the best remedy for self-pity was to turn it outward and help someone else. To Faye it was more than a glib homily to be spouted at pulpits, it was a maxim she had actually incorporated into her life—something I had seen practiced on dozens of occasions, including last Christmas when Faye had chaired her sorority's Sub-for-Santa. Christmas Day we delivered a carload of gifts to a needy family. It was this compassion, perhaps, that allowed her to initially see past the humble surroundings of my life.

She checked for her pocketbook, then hailed the next passing cab and took a ride into downtown Baltimore. Two hours later a taxi dropped her off in front of Canelli's. She was carrying two large plastic bags.

The restaurant was loud, the most crowded Faye had seen it in all her visits. Every table was taken and the lobby was full with a large number of foreign students celebrating the break. There were only two harried waitresses on, running from table to table, delivering pitchers of beer and pizzas as fast as the kitchen's brick oven could turn them out. The Please Wait To Be Seated sign was up; Faye peered around the corner into the dining room, looking for the little girl. She was nowhere in sight, though Faye was not surprised. With tables at a premium she was probably somewhere in the back of the restaurant with a box of crayons and take-out menus to color. Faye lay her sacks at her feet and stood near the front counter until a waitress approached. The young woman was tall with blonde-streaked brown hair, pulled back tightly, revealing the perspiration beaded on her forehead. Faye knew most of Canelli's waitresses by now, though with the exception of Judy, only by sight. The waitress reached for a pen, glancing down at the waiting list resting on the ledge below her. "Just one tonight?"

"Actually, I'm not here to eat. Is Judy working tonight?"

"Honey, I wish. She called in sick."

Faye's brow furrowed. "Does she live around here?"

"I think so. She walks to work with her little girl."

"Do you think I could get her address?"

The waitress grimaced. "I'd like to, but

I'm really busy. I don't think we can give out that information, anyway."

Faye frowned, glancing about as she considered her next move. "I brought these things for her daughter's Christmas."

The woman looked down at the bags at Faye's feet. A vestige of holiday spirit pried open her reserve. "All right. I'll check." She walked back through the swinging doors to the kitchen. A few minutes later she emerged carrying a tray. "I'll be right with you," she said as she passed.

She distributed the tray's contents then disappeared back into the kitchen. She returned a moment later holding a take-out menu. "Sorry that took so long. For some reason we don't have a job employment sheet on her. But one of the cooks knew where she lives. He drew this." She offered Faye a crude map scrawled in blue ink on the back of a menu. "He didn't know the address, but he says it's the gray house kitty-corner from the BP. There you are."

Faye glanced at the map then back up. "Thank you. And Merry Christmas."

She smiled. "Same to you."

Faye stowed the map in her coat pocket, lifted her bags, and left the restaurant. It had begun to snow again, though only lightly, and as she walked the pleasure of what she was doing began to warm her. She found herself walking very quickly. After two blocks she stopped, set her bags down in a blackened store entrance, and consulted her map. At the next corner she turned east, walking three blocks into a run-down neighborhood—the kind of neighborhood where rent was collected daily. In less focused times she would likely have considered taking such an excursion alone foolhardy, but beneath the falling snow the neighborhood did not look threatening. The snow blanketed the street, leaving it serene and peaceful.

Two blocks from the corner she spotted the backlit, emerald green signage of the BP. Across the street from it was a tiny house with steel gray shutters and cement steps leading upward to its covered porch. There were no lights visible from the street, inside or out.

Faye examined the house from the sidewalk, then walked to its front door, eager to lay down her bags. There was no doorbell, so she rapped on the aluminum of the storm door. Her knock was muffled by the leather gloves she wore. There was no reply. She knocked again, but was answered with the same silence. She tested the outer door and found that it was locked. She sat down on the top step, tired from her walk, wondering what to do with her packages. Her breath froze in the frigid air. Someone across the street looked out of their house at her, then drew the blind.

Faye sighed. She lifted her bags then walked around the house to see if there was a car or illuminated back light, any sign of occupancy. Around the side of the home there was a cracked cement stairway with a wrought-iron railing that led to a basement door. There was a simple light fixture above the door, but the bulb was missing, leaving it black in the bottom of the stairwell. The stairs were crusted with snow and ice. There were no footprints. If someone did live down there, they had not been in or out all day. Faye set her bags down at the top of the stairs and cautiously descended, holding fast to the cold, chipped railing. The doorbell was covered with a piece of masking tape that read in smeared pen, *Out of Order.* She knocked on the door. There were no sounds of movement inside. Faye pulled her coat tighter around herself, waited a moment, then removed her glove and pounded again, still harder. She replaced her glove and was about to abandon her quest when she heard the sliding of a dead bolt. The door opened a crack, then as wide as the brass chain of the door lock allowed. The pale-faced waitress peered out, her eyes both wide and stern.

"Who's there?"

"It's me, Faye Murrow. From the restaurant." Faye's breath froze in the air.

The slice of a face warily eyed her caller. "What do you want?"

"I brought something for your little girl—for Christmas."

The waitress glanced at her, then down at her feet suspiciously.

Faye rubbed her hands together. "I left

everything at the top of the stairs. I didn't want to slip and fall."

The woman gazed a moment longer, then her voice softened. "Just a minute." The door closed, a chain slid, then the door opened. The waitress stood in the doorway, wearing a gray sweat suit. Faye felt suddenly awkward, realizing that despite the many times she had seen this woman, she didn't really know her at all.

"I'll get the bags." Faye walked back up. She managed to carry both bags in one hand as she carefully descended the steps, her free hand grasping the cold metal handrail.

"Come in," the waitress said. "It's cold out."

Faye stepped inside and the woman closed the door behind her. It was cold inside as well, Faye thought. And it smelled. Faye's pregnancy had made her sensitive to odors, and the pungency of the room was enough to make her nauseous. Had it been earlier in the pregnancy she would have likely thrown up; she considered the possibility that she still might. She breathed through her mouth. The waitress noticed her discomfort.

"What is your name?"

"It's Faye. And you're Judy," Faye said. The waitress nodded, though it somehow did not come across as a confirmation.

"I'm sorry about the smell. My landlord upstairs is from Bangladesh. He uses a lot of curry in his cooking. I think that's why he has trouble finding renters."

"It's okay," Faye said. She glanced around, forcing herself not to gape. The apartment was dim and austere, a single room divided at one end by a counter. Behind it was the kitchen, less than ten feet by six feet wide. The kitchen had a window, though it opened on a window well of corrugated steel. The east wall was lined with white enamel cabinets. They were old and were chipped and scratched, their wounds stained with rust.

There were not the plug-in accoutrements usually associated with a kitchen. There was an old bread box and a wicker basket that held a single banana, freckled and withered. In the corner of the kitchen was a round-top refrigerator—a short evolutionary step from a wooden icebox, standing upright next to the counter with a hot plate and a metal sink with a few dishes inside. There was no phone visible, though there was a small pad of paper and a pen and a large, well-worn Bible. The only item in the kitchen that looked born of the decade was a Mr. Coffee coffeemaker.

Between the living area and the kitchen were two doors, one slightly ajar, revealing a shallow closet. The other opened to a bathroom. There was a large hole in its hollow door, roughly the size of a fist. The eggshell white walls looked dirty in the dim light and were bare except for a few nails and naked picture hooks.

The furniture in the room consisted of a small round Formica-topped table with metal legs. It was surrounded by three chairs, two metal ones that matched the table and one of wood with a wicker seat and back.

Against the wall opposite the kitchen lay a mattress with a mauve wool blanket spread across it and two flat throw pillows, gold and threadbare. The furniture looked as though it had been salvaged from a curbside refuse pile.

The little girl was a lump on the mattress, the blanket gathered up around her tiny body. The pillows shielded her head.

In the corner of the large space, set in a coffee can, was their Christmas tree—a single pine branch, with aluminum foil twisted into stars, and angels and ornaments cut from cardboard and colored with crayon. A strand of popcorn wound around the branch.

"May I take your coat?"

Faye set down her bags then removed her coat, relinquishing it to her host.

"Would it be all right if I used your bathroom?"

"Of course. It's right there." She gestured toward the first door. "I think there's paper."

Inside the room, Faye turned on the light and locked the door behind herself. There was a bare cardboard tube on the tissue holder, but on the tank lid was a short stack of dinner napkins imprinted with the Canelli's logo. As she sat down her knee touched a plastic curtain that overhung the graying tub from rusted shower rings. Also on the shower pole were a pair of slacks and a blouse, still damp, laid across it to dry. She peeked around the curtain. Inside the tub was a small pile of dirty clothes.

When she emerged from the bathroom, the waitress was lying on the mattress next to her daughter.

"How did you find me?" she asked.

"One of the cooks said he knew where you lived. He drew this map." She reached for it, then remembered the map was stowed in her coat. "It's in my coat. They said you were sick."

"Sarah's sick. She's been running a fever." She touched her daughter. "I'll make us some coffee."

She leaned over and kissed the girl, then stood. The child's eyes were heavy, and closed after her mother left.

"Do you mind if I sit with her?" Faye asked.

She glanced down at her daughter, who

showed no reaction, then nodded. Faye sat down on the mattress at the girl's side, combing her matted hair back with her fingers. A few moments later the waitress brought two cups of coffee to the table. "Would you like anything in your coffee?"

"Maybe some sugar."

She brought out a small plastic cup filled with packets of sweeteners and salt and pepper, the same packets offered at the pizzeria. Faye looked into the girl's face. Her eyes were closing again. Faye gently pulled the blanket up to the child's chin. She rose, then said quietly, "Let me show you what I brought."

Faye retrieved the two sacks and carried them over to the table, her back toward the girl. She pulled out a child's pair of red woolen mittens with a matching hat and scarf, then a rectangular box, which she turned to expose the doll beneath its cellophane wrap. The waitress's eyes glistened.

"I thought she'd like that. She doesn't have one already, does she?" Faye suddenly felt foolish for asking. It was clear she didn't have anything.

"No. She doesn't," the woman answered simply.

"I also brought some little things. Some Play-Doh and Silly Putty. I know she likes to color, so I brought some markers. They're washable." Faye lifted out a large box of crayons and a stack of Sesame Street coloring books. "I thought she'd like these." She reached into the other sack. "There's a small roasted turkey breast here. Some candied yams and a can of cranberry sauce. Also some cookies and a tin of cocoa."

The waitress's head dropped into her hands and her eyes filled with tears. Faye reached out and took her hand. The waitress lifted Faye's hand to her mouth and kissed it.

"Thank you."

"You're welcome."

"You carried all that all the way here?"

"Yes," Faye said lightly. "I'm glad you were home. My arms were ready to fall off."

With the back of her hand the waitress wiped the tears that rolled down her cheeks. Then she looked into Faye's eyes. "What am I to you?"

Faye considered the question. "What did Dickens say about the season? It's the one time we see each other for who we truly are, fellow passengers to the grave?"

The woman was quiet for a moment, then her countenance lightened.

"It's been so long since I've had someone to talk to. I don't know who to trust anymore. I've been afraid for so long."

"Why are you afraid?"

The waitress rubbed her forehead, started to open her mouth, then hesitated, as if resisting the temptation to speak.

"What's wrong, Judy?"

The waitress looked carefully at Faye, then said, "My name's not really Judy. I only use that name because there's a warrant out for my arrest."

CHAPTER FOURTEEN
The Fugitive

*There are times when doing
what is right and avoiding the
appearance of evil are not the
same thing.*

MICHAEL KEDDINGTON'S JOURNAL

It was hard to believe that this young mother could be guilty of anything greater than tearing the manufacturer's label off of a mattress. It was not until she had absorbed the meaning of the confession that Faye spoke.

"What is your real name?" she asked.

"Hallie," the waitress said, then repeated it just for the amusement of it. "Hallie. It's been a while since I said that. It's odd to me that you can take something so basic to your being as your name and just discard it. I don't think you can do that without changing yourself. I tried to change Sarah's name, but it was too hard for her. Whenever someone asked her her name she would tell people that her name *used* to be Sarah. It caused more problems than it solved."

"What did you do?" Faye asked more cautiously.

Hallie turned her face toward the little girl. "I took Sarah from her father. They say I kidnapped her." She looked back. "But we had to run."

"From where?"

"Home was Alabama. Before everything went insane."

"What happened?"

She was quiet for a moment, staring at her coffee. She stirred it gently. "I was married for seven years. He was the kind of man every woman thinks she wants to marry. He was a successful lawyer. A partner in his firm. Handsome. Turned heads wherever he went. The kind of grin people go to movies to see.

"He was from a wealthy family with political clout. His grandfather had been the speaker of the Alabama House. His father was a powerful lobbyist. He had political aspirations. I was from nowhere—a little farming community. My whole married life everyone told me how lucky I was to be married to him. I thought I was lucky, not because he was rich or anything, but because I loved him." She looked up at Faye, her eyebrows knit in distress. "They say hardship can make or break a relationship. I ended up on the wrong side of that coin. He lost interest in me when I was diagnosed with multiple sclerosis."

Faye looked at her quizzically. "You have MS?"

"For eleven years."

"Eleven years," Faye repeated as if in disbelief.

"That's when I first started noticing the symptoms. MS doesn't throw you in a wheelchair overnight. It's usually a pretty slow-moving disease. It's like your body uses guerrilla warfare on itself. It hits you for a while then it goes away. They're called exasperations. I had it for eight years before they finally took an MRI and found lesions on my brain. It was the day before Sarah's third birthday. Before that I had gone to about a dozen different specialists. They diagnosed it as everything

from chronic fatigue syndrome to hypo-
glycemia."

"When did you figure it out?"

"I was reading an article about Annette
Funicello. As she described her MS symptoms I recognized them all. My hands and
feet were numb all the time. Numb and
cold. I couldn't stand hot baths. Southern
summers about did me in. I had paresthesias."

"What's paresthesias?"

She looked at Faye and smiled. "I guess
I'm teaching the medical student. It's that
pins-and-needles feeling." Faye nodded.
"It's been hard. I heard someone describe
MS as the junk God had left over from all
the other diseases. Two years ago I went
color-blind. Just recently I've lost the
strength in my arms. That's the way MS is,"
she said, and she rubbed her hands together as if she were suddenly reminded of
their numbness. "I always thought if you
could get through life without contracting
a disease that had its own telethon you
were doing okay."

"Is that why you dropped the tray?"

"I've dropped a lot of trays. That was a bad day."

"So your husband just left you?"

"Not at first. It was gradual. I was his second wife. The newer model, some said. He was twelve years older than me. He started working more, staying out later. I heard rumors that he had girls on the side. I knew he did. A woman just knows these things. Sometimes she hides her head in the sand to protect her heart, or her home, but she knows. People would stop talking when I would walk into a room. I found a lipstick case in his suit.

"One night he came home really late. It was past three. I asked him where he'd been, expecting his usual excuse, hard at work, providing for Sarah and me. Instead he said he needed time alone to think about things. He confessed to being with another woman. He didn't say much more than that." She looked at Faye, and there was a peculiar glint in her eye. "I went crazy. I started hitting him. It was bad enough that he was doing it, but to rub my face in it, then hold me out as if I was being weighed in the balance, I couldn't stand it. I told him to get out. The next day we separated."

She took a deep breath. "I didn't see him for a while. I guessed he was out sowing his oats. A few months after that our divorce came through. It was pretty congenial. No big fights over custody or anything. I wanted him to see Sarah, she needed that, I thought. A girl needs a father.

"Then, six months later, totally out of the blue he started to call. At first I would just hang up on him. But he persevered. He became really humble." A subtle grin played on her lips. "A quality I've always liked in a man."

"A rare quality," Faye said.

"It was like the man I had fallen in love with was back. He would be really sweet. He sent me flowers. He would say things like he never really deserved me. He seemed actually interested in me and what I needed. He even offered to watch Sarah so I could go out. He used to be gone so much and pay so little attention to her. I was so pleased. I thought maybe some conscience had kicked in and he was going to be a real father. I started going out, not much, just playing bridge with my friends or going to a Bible class down at the church, and he'd come over and watch her. He said he wanted to prove himself. It was too good to be true. I actually started considering asking him to come back.

"Then one night I came home from playing bridge and he was acting really strange. He couldn't get out of the house fast enough. Sarah was crying and wouldn't stop. He called her a brat. That night she woke up screaming." As she recalled the moment, Hallie's voice faltered. Faye took her hand. "She was saying, 'No, Daddy. Stop. It hurts.' The next day I took her to our doctor. He checked her. At first he said she'd been violated. Then he left the room for a while and when he came back he said he wasn't sure.

"I didn't know what to do. I turned him in to the state, I told the caseworker everything. They went out to see him but nothing ever came of it. They believed what he told them, that I was a vindictive ex. Afterward he called and said if I ever tried something like that again he would get me committed to an insane asylum and take full custody of Sarah. After what he had already gotten away with, why wouldn't I believe him? I was so afraid of him and all his connections. I took a chance anyway. I filed for sole custody of Sarah. But he won again. They granted him continued unsupervised visits.

"Then I learned that he was HIV-positive. I don't know where he got it. I had heard rumors he had been with prostitutes. I had myself and Sarah checked, but we were negative. I couldn't take the chance of Sarah being abused again. We picked up in the middle of the night and left everything behind. We've been on the road ever since."

"How long ago was that?"

"Seventeen months."

"How have you survived?"

"I had some money from the divorce, but that ran out about eight months ago. I saw it coming, that's why I got a job as a waitress. I made a deal with the night manager,

I would work for tips and he wouldn't have to pay me or register me as an employee." The passion suddenly left her voice and she again focused on her coffee. "If I'm discovered they'll take Sarah away. I'll go to jail and she'll go to her father. It could be her death sentence."

"Does anyone know where you are?"

"You." She shook her head slowly. "No. Not even my parents."

"That's why you couldn't report the man harassing you."

"He's the night manager. Craig. He knows I have a secret. It wouldn't take a brain surgeon to figure that out."

They were both quiet for a while, the silence interrupted only by the upstairs arrival of her landlord. Finally Hallie said, "I'm sorry to turn this into a pity party. You haven't told me anything about yourself. Why aren't you going home for school break?"

"They misbooked my flight. I'm leaving tomorrow."

"Where's home?"

"Ogden, Utah. I'm sure you haven't heard of it. It's just north of Salt Lake City."

"You're a first-year student?"

"First. Maybe my last."

"What do you mean?"

"I found out a couple months ago that I'm pregnant. If," Faye corrected herself, *"when* my father finds out, he'll cut off the money for school."

Hallie glanced down at Faye's barren ring finger. "Where's the father?"

"He's back in Utah. We're married. We secretly eloped before I came out. My father doesn't approve of him."

"We all have our crosses," Hallie said.

Faye felt embarrassed to have her adversity likened to Hallie's. "No, you have a cross. I have a detour."

For a moment the two women stared into each other's eyes. Finally Faye said, "I better go. Is there anything I can do for you?"

Hallie shook her head. "You've done so much by coming here tonight. I don't know how I can repay you."

"It's been its own reward. I'll see you when I come back."

"Thank you."

The women stood. Hallie noticed her little girl's eyes were open. "Sarah, honey. Can you tell Faye thank you?"

The little girl squinted. She said in a small voice, half whispered, "You said not to talk to her."

Hallie said, "It's okay now. She's a friend."

The little girl smiled. "Good," she said. "Thank you."

At the doorway Faye remembered something. She reached into her besom pocket and brought out a small change purse. She extracted from it a folded one-hundred-dollar bill and handed it to Hallie. "Here. My dad gave me that as a security blanket. I think you could put it to better use than me."

She took the money and embraced Faye. Then she began to cry, and this time she wept openly. "Thank you, Faye. Thank God for you."

"Merry Christmas," Faye said. She kissed her cheek. Then she pulled her coat tightly around herself and started the long walk back to the dorm. Her mind was full with another's joy and travail, and she had nearly forgotten the reason she had thought to go there in the first place.

CHAPTER FIFTEEN

Christmas Break

Faye arrived home tonight for Christmas. Absence may make the heart grow fragile.

MICHAEL KEDDINGTON'S JOURNAL

There are two places to avoid the week before Christmas: shopping malls and airports. Faye's flight touched down around eight-twenty Saturday evening, two days before Christmas. It was fortunate that I had planned to arrive forty minutes early, as it took me nearly an hour just to find a parking space in the short-term parking terrace. Had Faye's flight not been a half hour late I would have missed her arrival.

I parked my car and fought my way through the crowds. I stopped at a row of monitors to check for her gate number, and only when I saw her flight was delayed did I breathe easier. I suppose I had never been so anxious to see someone in my entire life.

As I walked into the crowded gate area I saw Dr. Murrow sitting at the end of a row of black vinyl chairs buried beneath the spread of a *USA Today*. I was not surprised to see him. Faye, with her usual tact, had warned me that he would be there. He glanced up at me only briefly, acknowledging me with no more familiarity than any stranger in the flow of holiday travelers. I found a seat at the opposite end of the gate and waited. When the arrival of the flight was announced, we both stood and walked to the end of the carpet next to the gate agent.

Judging from the way Dr. Murrow jockeyed for position, it was clear to me how important it was to him that Faye acknowledge him first. I stepped back. The jetway door was opened and the passengers poured forth in a great torrent, flowing around us like two rocks set in a stream. At that moment I had a thought born of panic: *What if she was showing?* There would be a sizable audience for the showdown.

Just then Faye stepped from the jetway. My heart leapt at the sight of her. Somehow

I always forgot how beautiful she was, as if my mind refused to accept that such a woman could choose to align herself with me. Her hair was slightly shorter than when she had left and her face was slightly fuller, though that was as likely attributable to cafeteria food as pregnancy. She was wearing a coat and a loose-fitting tunic. If she was showing at all it was well concealed beneath her attire. She had two bags: a wheeled hunter green carry-on which she pulled from its extended handle and a glossy shopping bag from Saks. She glanced about looking for a familiar face.

When she saw her father she went to him, dropped her carry-ons, and they embraced. She then saw me, came over, and threw her arms around my neck and kissed me. She did not let go. As joyful as our reunion was, there was a solemnness to her demeanor, as if in anticipation of the unfinished business the week held. We parted and she stood there glancing between the two of us.

"How was your flight?" I asked.

"It was good. The landing was something else. I don't know if we landed or were shot down."

"Do you have luggage?" the doctor asked.

"Just my carry-ons."

He reached for her rolling bag and the twine handles of the Saks bag, signaling his intention to drive her home.

"Dad, I'm going to ride back with Michael."

He made no effort to conceal his displeasure. "Your mother has dinner waiting for you. Are you coming straight home?"

"We'll be right there."

I'm certain that he was not pleased with the "we," but he held his tongue.

Dr. Murrow carried Faye's luggage as the three of us walked out to the parking terrace. Faye kissed her father good-bye, then we climbed two levels to my car. I unlocked and opened the door for her. When I got in the other side Faye sat quietly. I leaned over and we kissed, but it did not seem natural. There was an awkward tension between us, perhaps less of excitement than expectation. I sat back in my seat. "I've missed you so much."

She smiled sadly. "Me too."

"You're not showing."

She glanced down at her waist, fingered her waistband beneath the tunic. "My pants are tight. It's noticeable if you look close enough."

"You look beautiful," I said.

At that she turned away and I did not understand why. I started up the car, revved its engine against the cold, then pulled out of the parking terrace to the exit gate below. I handed the man at the toll booth two dollars. As the gate arm raised Faye said, "I'm going to have to tell my parents. This week."

The traffic from the gates and the terminal curbs combined ahead into a two-lane highway. I mentally shelved Faye's news to focus on the road until we had merged left toward the I-15 turnoff. "Why this week?"

"I owe them that.'"

"Have you told anyone else?"

"My roommates know. Also Mr. Cambridge, the dean of student affairs."

"What was his response?"

"He was understanding. It's not the first time it's happened."

"So when do we tell them?"

"Not *we*. There's no point in you being there. It will just make things worse."

"You're carrying our baby. It's only right that I'm there."

Faye didn't respond to my challenge. We were both silent for a while, and the sound of the road dominated the cabin. "The day after Christmas," she suddenly said. "There's no sense ruining Christmas for everybody."

I reached over and took her hand. She began to cry.

"Michael, I'm not ready to be a mother. And I feel so guilty that I don't want this baby. Lou Dean and Angel keep trying to talk me into getting an abortion." She gazed out the window. Then she said softly, almost to herself, "What were we thinking?"

"What do you mean?"

Faye didn't answer and her silence cut as deeply as her words. It was as if she'd dropped a wrecking ball on my unsuspecting heart. I grew angrier as my hurt intensified. "I don't know what you were thinking, but I was thinking that I loved you. And that I wanted to spend the rest of my life with you."

She still didn't answer. Neither of us spoke the rest of the way back to Ogden. We arrived at Faye's home and I parked in her driveway. I left the car idling. For four months I had counted the minutes until Faye's return, and within thirty minutes of her arrival we weren't speaking to each other. We both sat there for a while, then she unlatched her door. "Come on, Michael."

I didn't move and she turned back to me. "Are you coming?"

"No."

She lowered her head. "I'm sorry I said that. I'm just under a lot of pressure."

"I understand pressure, Faye. But we can let it bring us together or tear us apart. We're far enough apart already."

She took a deep breath, then looked at me with pleading eyes. "Please don't leave me tonight."

Just then the home's front door opened. Abigail came running out, her face lit with excitement. "Faye! Faye!"

She looked back at me. Her voice became more contrite. "I know it was a terrible thing to say. Please, Michael."

I exhaled, then relented and shut off the car. Faye opened her own door and climbed out. I followed her.

Faye's ability to mask her feelings was remarkable. She was met by her entire family in the foyer. After the initial greetings, Mrs. Murrow directed everyone to the dining room. Dinner was on the table, except for the things she had placed back in the oven to keep warm. There was a place setting for me, though I suspect it had only been set when the doctor had informed her that I was driving Faye home. Though Faye had already eaten on the plane, she ate again.

After dinner we all sat in the living room and talked until late. By eleven o'clock the fatigue was showing on Faye's face. I suppose we had conveniently forgotten that, to her, it was one in the morning. I excused myself, and Faye walked me out, followed only by Abigail.

"You've had a long day," I said.

"It feels like a week."

Abigail said, "Will you sleep in my bedroom tonight?"

"I was planning on it. Now go inside."

Abigail looked at me and smiled. "Bye, Michael."

"Bye, Abby."

Faye walked me out to the car. She was in better spirits than she had arrived in. She pressed her body into mine, and for the first time I noticed the subtle changes the pregnancy had wrought in her form. "I wish you didn't have to work tomorrow. Are you really working a double shift?"

"It was the only way I could get the next two days off."

"Will you still come to midnight mass?"

"I'm planning on it, but I don't know if I can get off early. I'll have to meet you at the church. Save me a seat."

I kissed her, and this time we kissed at length. When we finished she bowed her head slightly. "I really am sorry about

what I said on the way home from the airport."

I said nothing. The wound was still too
raw to absolve her of blame so quickly.

Faye sensed my hesitancy. "You're the
most important person in my life. I love
you with all of my heart." At that she kissed
me again, then she shivered. "I'm freezing."

"You better get inside," I said.

I climbed in the car while she ran back to
the warmth of the house. As I drove home I
wondered how to bandage my heart.

I do not care much for snow except for
one day of the year: Christmas Eve. I was
not disappointed this season and the flakes
fell as if on cue. Shortly after noon, a light
snowfall commenced and continued its
silent descent until the remnant snow of
the week before was concealed beneath a
milky new blanket of white.

The Arcadia was bright, alive with excitement of the holiday and the arrival of
families, come to take their parents and
grandparents home for the festivities. I had
just returned from helping a resident out to

a car when Sharon caught up with me. "Would you stop in and see what you can do with Agnes and Wendell?"

"What's up?"

"They're having marital problems. She just asked me to help her file for divorce. She's demanding that he move out of her room immediately. Wendell thinks he has to sleep in the hall."

Agnes and Wendell's room was located at the far end of the west wing. When I arrived, their door was slightly ajar and I knocked on it as I pushed it open. It was quite a sight. Wendell sat on the floor wearing pajamas and a red-and-green-striped Christmas cap. He was packing all his worldly possessions into a single cardboard box. Agnes sat in the west corner of the room icily watching him, motionless in a rocking chair. She was wearing a red dress with a white faux-fur collar and sleeves. She looked like a malevolent Mrs. Claus, her prunish face twisted with contempt.

"Going someplace?" I asked.

Wendell looked up at me, his eyebrows

low above his eyes like great, gray caterpillars. "Agnes has thrown me out. She wants a divorce."

I turned toward her. "You're not serious about getting a divorce?"

"What?"

I said louder, "You're not really getting a divorce?"

"Why wouldn't we?"

"You're in your nineties. It's a little late for fresh starts."

"It's never too late to do the right thing," she snapped.

Wendell looked at me helplessly.

"So what brought this on?"

"What?"

"What brought this on?" I shouted.

"I caught him with another woman."

I looked at Wendell in bewilderment. "Doing what?"

Her eyes narrowed in bitter remembrance. "They were holding hands."

I forced myself not to smile. "For that you're going to end seventy years of marriage? Come on you two, it's Christmas Eve."

Wendell scowled. "Well, I ain't givin' her nuthin' this year. Woman didn't use what I gave her last Christmas."

She glared at him. "What did he say?"

"He said you didn't use what he gave you last Christmas," I shouted.

This made her face twist still tighter. I turned to him. "What did you give her?"

"A cemetery plot."

I bit my tongue until I could speak without laughing. "I suggest you two try to work this out. In the meantime there are no extra rooms and Wendell cannot sleep in the hall. So unless you can find another couple willing to split up, you're stuck with each other."

"What did he say?" Agnes asked.

Wendell hollered, "He said you're stuck with me 'cause there's no room in the inn."

"Then find a manger."

Thanks to Brent, and a light workload, I got off work at 11:30. Brent had his moments. I drove across town on slick streets to the Church of the Madeleine. The parking lot and nearby streets were full of cars, and the first available place to park was four blocks from the church.

The night was a memorable seduction of the senses, though I suppose I experienced it not so much in its own right as in its expression through Faye. The church was crowded and fairly resonated with piousness, as the worshipers were both excited and reverent.

Inside the main hall there was a wooden crèche arranged beside a confessional. To the right of it, next to another confessional, were several rows of candles. Before us was the sanctuary with the tabernacle and an altar, covered with a linen cloth and sewn with the word "Sanctus." Behind us was a choir loft with an arched ceiling with words inscribed in gold leaf, THIS IS THE HOUSE OF GOD AND THE GATE TO HEAVEN.

I found the Murrows seated on a pew four rows from the back of the church. Faye smiled when she saw me and I squeezed in next to her, pressed tightly between Faye and the end of the pew. Jayne sat on Faye's right and held her hand. The choir had already begun singing traditional carols; the congregation joined in. After a few numbers, the congregation dropped out and the choir sang alone the "Resonet in Laudibus" and "Puer Natus in Bethlehem." This was followed by the mass.

There came a large procession consisting of an incense carrier followed by candle holders, the carrier of the Crucifix, the carrier of the infant Jesus, and finally the priest. The priest placed the infant in the manger, blessed the crèche and all those who prayed in front of it, then walked to the altar where he removed his cope and was helped into his mass vestment.

Faye was radiant. I noticed that her gaze was not set on the procession, but on the crèche, her eyes fixed on Mary kneeling next to the manger. I had never before considered the deeper meaning Christmas has for mothers. I have no doubt that Faye was having that experience, falling into the realization that all women experience Christmas differently once they've known childbirth: that pomp and pageantry aside, the nativity was still the story of a mother and a baby.

There was peace there that night and even Dr. Murrow seemed not to mind my participation. This didn't surprise me. I had learned before that the church was a sanctuary and that like many other men, Dr. Murrow was a better Christian inside the church than out of it.

The ceremony took just less than an hour, but with the crowds and traffic I didn't arrive home until two. I slept in the next morning until Faye called to wish me a Merry Christmas.

CHAPTER SIXTEEN
The Calm

I am grateful for the
Christmases of my life.

MICHAEL KEDDINGTON'S JOURNAL

I did not go directly to Faye's house. I drove to the cemetery and walked through shin-deep snow to my mother's grave carrying two potted poinsettias. My mother had loved flowers, and though I guess a poinsettia is not technically a flower, at Christmastime it was her favorite. She liked to tell me that its shape was symbolic of the Star of Bethlehem and its red leaves were symbolic of the blood of the Christmas child.

I knelt down in the snow next to her headstone, set one of the plants to the side, and pushed the other deep into the snow covering my mother's grave. The crimson leaves blazed against the luminous backdrop of white. I said a prayer, and as I did I felt that warmth I often did at her grave. "Next Christmas," I said, "I'll bring your grandchild."

I left the second plant at Esther's grave. Like my mother, there were never flowers at her grave unless I brought them. She had no one to visit her but me.

I arrived at the Murrow home as the sisters were opening the last of their presents. The whole family was assembled in the living room. Dr. Murrow sat in his La-Z-Boy across from his wife, watching the event with a cup of Irish coffee in one hand and an opened can of Almond Roca candy on the table next to him. I had brought gifts which I dispersed upon my arrival, with the exception of Faye's. Exchanging gifts was a ritual we left for when we were alone.

I gave Abigail a backpack for school and a Paula Abdul dance video. For Jayne I had a music book with guitar music and a George Michael cassette tape. She smiled and hugged me. I was pleased to see her so animated. When all the presents were opened Dr. Murrow disappeared to his den and Faye and Abigail went in to help their mother prepare supper. When we were alone I asked Jayne how she was doing.

"I've got it all figured out," she said. "Let's go up to my room and listen to my tape."

By noon the dining room table was set with the kind of spread Mrs. Murrow was famous for: sugar-crusted ham, sliced turkey, mashed potatoes, Parker House rolls, asparagus tips, sugar-basted acorn squash. There were two kinds of pie for dessert, mincemeat and pumpkin. Mrs. Murrow could make even mincemeat appetizing. We all sat down. Dr. Murrow offered a lengthy blessing, then we descended upon the food. In a home of females they marveled at how much I ate, though it clearly pleased Mrs. Murrow. To the cook, indulgence, not imitation, is the sincerest form of flattery. I ate too much, but without regret.

After dinner Faye insisted that she and her mother do the dishes while I retire to the family room with her father. I sensed that this was a conspiracy of sorts.

There is an old adage about sin. First we abhor it, then pity it, then embrace it. I suppose Faye's was a conspiracy along those lines. As Dr. Murrow clearly abhorred me, Faye reasoned that maybe, given enough time and exposure, he might move on to pitying me. Hardly flattering, but a start. Or at least I suppose that was the idea.

The truth is I would have rather helped in the kitchen, but Faye had already set her mind, so I joined the doctor in the den. Dr. Murrow turned on the television and we both sat there in silence watching him finger the remote, surfing the channels until he concluded that nothing was on worth watching. He turned off the television and walked out of the room as if he'd been alone.

I retrieved the remote and ended up watching the last half hour of *It's a Wonderful Life*, and the first hour of *Miracle on 34th Street* starring Maureen O'Hara. Jayne came in and joined me for the second movie and was still watching after I left with Faye.

As a bachelor, I did not understand Faye and her mother's method of washing dishes. They would wash, scrub, and rinse the dinnerware before putting it into the dishwasher. My feeling has always been that if you're not sure whether or not a dish is dirty, it isn't. Of course, like many men, I also believe a shirt left in the dirty clothes pile gets cleaner by the day. Left long enough, washing it became unnecessary. But I digress.

Mrs. Murrow rinsed the dishes while Faye stacked them in the dishwasher.

"How's Jayne doing?" Faye asked.

Mrs. Murrow's brow furrowed. "Did Michael tell you?"

"Tell me what?"

"That Jayne's been having a hard time."

"No."

"Well, there's no need to worry about it anymore. She's doing all right now. Finally."

Now Faye *was* worried.

"What do you mean? What's been going on?"

"You might as well know." She glanced around to make sure that they were alone. "She's been so moody lately that no one can stand to be around her."

"That doesn't sound like Jayne."

"Well, she's a teenager. You know how it is. It's a hormonal roller coaster. One of her friends gets upset about something and it's the end of the world. And then there's school. She dropped calculus without telling us. Her grades have fallen. Her last report card she had a B average. She got her first C. I don't think you ever got below a B plus, did you?"

Faye didn't answer the question. "What did Dad do?"

"He gave it to her. Said if her grades don't go up he's taking away her stereo and driving privileges."

"Did it work?"

"We'll see. We'll get her report card in a couple weeks. Anyway, it hasn't stopped her from acting so peculiarly. Almost every night she comes home from school and sits in her bedroom and listens to her music with those headphones on." She added, "I really wish Michael hadn't given her another tape."

"That's what I told him to get," Faye said. "It's what Jayne said she wanted."

"Most of the time I don't even see her before she goes to bed. A few weeks ago we sat her down and asked her if she was using drugs. She said she wasn't. While she was at school I went through her room and drawers with a fine-tooth comb. I didn't find anything. At least not drugs."

"Why didn't you tell me about this?"

"You don't need more to worry about."

"What else is she doing?"

"Little things. Amanda invited her to an overnight ski party at Park City and she turned her down."

"Jayne turned down a ski trip?"

Her mother sensed her concern and tried to assuage it. "You went through your times too. You carried the world on your shoulders. It's your father's legacy."

"Thank you, Dad."

"I was concerned that she would ruin

Christmas. But, thankfully, the last few days she's come out of it."

"Why the sudden change?"

"I don't know." She handed Faye a dish. "Maybe because she knew you were coming home."

Faye frowned.

"Now don't worry, honey. The teenage years are hard. That's what being a teenager is all about."

"I think that's what life's about."

Mrs. Murrow smiled. "Like I said, she does seem to be coming out of it. I went upstairs yesterday and her room was clean. Really clean. Everything was put away in its place. I don't remember the last time that happened without coercion. In fact, a couple days ago she gave Abigail her guitar. She's finally thinking about someone besides herself."

"She gave away her guitar?"

"She tried. Abigail wouldn't take it."

Faye was puzzled. "That's odd."

"I think it was very generous. You know how much that guitar means to her." Mrs.

Murrow wiped her hands with a dishcloth. "How are you feeling, dear?"

"I'm fine."

"Are you?"

Faye looked carefully at her mother, then smiled, trying to guess her mother's intent. "Why do you ask?"

"I've just noticed that you seem tired. Are you gaining weight?"

"A little. It's hard to find time to exercise."

Mrs. Murrow just nodded, though Faye wondered if she suspected. Then she said, as if in resolution, "It's been good having you home."

"It's been a good break. There's no place like home for the holidays."

Her mother sang the refrain, "There's no place like home for the holidays . . ."

Faye smiled. "I guess I've been pretty homesick. Fortunately school's so busy it helps me keep my mind off home." She stooped over to arrange a handful of utensils in the dishwasher. "How's Abigail?"

"Same as always. A rocket in a girl's body."

"And Dad?"

"He's still worried about you and Michael. I'm sure he thought you'd be through with him by now."

Faye stood up from the dishwasher and faced her mother. "I love Michael with all my heart. Dad's going to have to learn to accept him."

"It's just a father thing. You're his first and he wants the best for you."

"Michael *is* the best for me."

"How is Michael doing?"

"Michael always does well at school. He ought to be the one at Johns Hopkins. Except he prefers literature to chemistry. He'll make a good lawyer." Faye closed the dishwasher.

"Is that what he's planning to do now? Don't tell your father. He'll really think he has reason to dislike him."

When the kitchen was clean, Faye found me in the den. She took my hand and led me to the living room where we sat alone on the littered carpet next to the tree. There was still a pile of unopened presents. Faye pushed them my way.

As I started to open the first gift Faye said, "That's from my parents. Well, my mother," she said, shrugging. "I helped her with sizes."

I opened the box. There was a polo shirt and V-necked sweater from Nordstrom's. Faye gave me a sweatshirt imprinted with JOHNS HOPKINS UNIVERSITY, a pair of Ray-Ban Wayfarers, a gift certificate to a bookstore, cassette tapes of the B-52's and Culture Club, a pair of acid-washed jeans, and a stack of shirts. Faye liked to dress me.

Then I handed her her gifts. The first was a book of one hundred classic love poems. I also gave her a gold bracelet that matched the locket I had given her last Christmas. We laughed, looking back on that painful day, as she had expected a ring instead of a locket.

Finally she opened my last gift to her— the one I was most excited to share. She unwrapped the box, freeing from the packing tissue a small porcelain carousel music box. She carefully lifted it out.

"I thought you might like to take your carousel back to Baltimore," I said.

Faye smiled then kissed me. "I love it." She wound its key. The carousel began to turn, its music box playing to the tune of "Raindrops Keep Falling on My Head." She set it aside then leaned back against the couch, next to the manteled fireplace, motioning for me to join her. I lay my head in her lap and she gently combed her fingers through my hair. It was ecstasy being alone with her. I should have known it could not last.

Faye had too many friends. News was out that Faye was in town, and as the day waned they began to descend upon the house, trickling in at first in ones and twos, then in an interminable stream of girl-friends and sorority sisters. By twilight the home was crowded, as if a party had spontaneously combusted at the Murrows'. Despite her fatigue and our desire to be alone, Faye was happy. At least she was until Shandra's announcement.

There were at least a dozen of Faye's friends milling about the living room when word went out that Shandra had an announcement to make and everyone congregated around her.

Shandra was expecting. The crowd broke into cheers and applause. Shandra gushed and received congratulations like a Miss America surrounded by envious also-rans. At the height of the celebration I looked over at Faye. She had quietly stepped back from the fray and stood alone against the wall. A fabricated smile stretched across her face. Even though Faye and Shandra had embraced, I could tell that Faye was hurting. Whether Shandra's pregnancy woke Faye to a remembrance of her own or angered her that her news would not be met with such joy, I didn't know. Maybe neither. But her mood changed and she was sullen and introspective, even after they had all left. It was dark by that time, past ten. I did not ask her how she felt. It was obvious. I carried my presents out to my car and went home alone.

CHAPTER SEVENTEEN
The Storm

Life, as I knew it, ended today.

MICHAEL KEDDINGTON'S JOURNAL

Faye arrived at my place the next morning by dawn. I woke early, anticipating her arrival. I was making hot chocolate and toast about the time she arrived. Breakfast went cold. We'd been apart for too long.

I gave her another present, something her family would not have appreciated. A spaghetti-strapped negligee. Faye made some disparaging comment about the size of her expanding abdomen, then quickly disappeared into the bathroom to try it on.

The sweetness of being together restored me, miraculously erasing whatever pain I had accrued during the weeks of her absence. That noon, bathed in afterglow, we lay in bed talking, the noon sun streaming in through our window, dividing the room.

"I don't know why men buy lingerie," she said. "All they want to do is remove it as quickly as possible."

"Same reason we wrap presents," I said.

She smiled at that. "Except men don't wrap presents. They leave them in the store sack or have someone else wrap them."

"That's not always true."

She lifted the sheer negligee from the floor by one finger. "Who wrapped this?"

"The lady at the store," I reluctantly admitted.

"My point," she said triumphantly. She suddenly looked down at herself. "Do I look fat?"

"No. Just starkly, painfully gorgeous."

She dismissed my compliment, running her fingers up her body. "I'm getting fat. My mother asked if I was putting on weight. I think she suspects." Her voice fell. "It doesn't matter. She'll know before much longer."

I caressed Faye's chin. "I've been thinking. We can do this. You don't have to quit school. I'll sell the house and move to Baltimore with you. We have the money Esther left me to help out. I've got more than five thousand dollars equity in this place and I've saved another thousand since summer. I'll find a job back there."

Faye didn't look hopeful. "You couldn't earn enough to pay for my schooling."

"So we'll get a student loan. Most med students take out loans."

"What about your schooling?"

"I've been on-again, off-again for three years already. A few more years won't hurt. And this way one of us will be with the baby." I lay my face against hers. "We can do it."

She was quiet again. "I'm just not ready for this."

I pulled Faye into me and held her against my chest and my racing heart. It was the calm before the storm. By evening her parents would know the truth about our marriage and Faye's pregnancy.

I would be lying to say I was not anxious. I have never enjoyed confrontation, but I do not fear it. At least not for myself. But I did for Faye. My insistence on being with her when she told her parents made her more fearful and I was now questioning whether my insistence was to support Faye or for my own pride and appearance. Maybe both. Still, I couldn't feel good about sending her into the lions' den alone. There was no knowing how far her father might take things. It was not outside the realm of possibility that he might disown her. We must have been having similar thoughts, for as I held her she began to tremble. She said softly, "It's been such a nice holiday. It's a pity to spoil it."

"Then don't tell them."

"I have to tell them."

I held her and she again buried her face in my chest.

"Everything will be okay," I said, caressing the back of her neck. Just then the phone rang. "Let it ring," I said.

On the seventh ring Faye grimaced. "It must be for me." I rolled over and lifted the receiver. There came an unfamiliar, terse voice.

"Is Faye Murrow there?"

"Yes, may I ask who's calling?"

"I'm Faye's aunt Geniel."

"Just a moment." I covered the mouthpiece. "It's for you."

"Who is it?"

"It's your aunt Geniel."

She raised her head. "My aunt?"

I set the phone between us, and Faye brought the receiver to her ear. "Hello." I watched as her demeanor turned from curiosity to horror. Her mouth opened as if to gasp. "We'll be right there." She sprung out of bed and began collecting her clothes. "Michael, we've got to get to McKay-Davis. Something's happened to Jayne."

I don't remember the drive, but I must have been flying. We arrived at the emergency wing of McKay-Davis hospital within ten minutes of the call. Inside the lobby, Faye's mother was standing next to a Catholic priest who was trying to console her. Another woman, whom I later learned was Faye's aunt, was holding Abigail. There were a handful of other friends or relatives there, as well as some of Dr. Murrow's associates from the hospital. I wondered at the number of people who had gathered. There was a panicked look in Faye's eyes.

"Where's Jayne?" Faye asked. "What's going on? Where's my father?"

A nurse was the first to reach her. "Dr. Murrow's in with Jayne."

Faye's speech was rapid. "Robin, what's happened?"

The nurse looked her in the eyes. "Jayne overdosed on pills."

Faye just stared at her as if she were deciphering a message in a foreign language.

"Overdosed? But she's okay, right?" She turned to me. "She's okay, they can pump her stomach. What kind of pills were they?"

Just then Dr. Murrow stepped from the double doors of the emergency room. He was crying. Mrs. Murrow looked up at him, her expression frozen in horror, as if understanding the unspoken verdict but unwilling to accept it. His voice was as dull as his eyes. "She's gone."

Mrs. Murrow shrieked. At that split second the world as I knew it stopped, the noise of the room coalesced into a surreal blur like the scratching of a vinyl record. Faye screamed, "No!" She began to tremble then to hyperventilate. She raised both her hands to her mouth and I reached out for her as she collapsed to the floor.

"Jayne! Oh, please God, no. Jayne's not dead. She's not dead." She looked at me and her eyes were wild and dark. "Do you hear me?! She's not dead! She's not dead!" Her voice began to crack. "Oh, don't let her be dead. She can't be dead."

The nurse and I crouched at her side and I held her. More than anything I wished that we could wake from this nightmare.

CHAPTER EIGHTEEN

The Funeral

If the road to Hell is paved with good intentions, we made one heck of a road crew.

MICHAEL KEDDINGTON'S JOURNAL

In the Arcadia, I had seen death prayed for, begged for, sometimes anticipated like some long-awaited excursion. I had seen families walk away from loved ones with red-rimmed eyes but hearts of peace murmuring that it was all for the best. My own mother's death I met with fierce resistance, but I eventually conceded that the cancer that had ravaged her body had made life too painful for her to endure. In the end I had hoped for her release.

Suicide wears a heavier cloak. It is a psychological land mine, killing, maiming, and scarring not just the hapless who tripped it, but all those in its vicinity.

The next week passed in an indescribable haze of pain. Every word Jayne had said, every hint so quickly passed over, was now recalled—glowing as bright as a branding iron. I wondered how we all could have been so blind.

Jayne had swallowed the contents of a nearly full bottle of Elavil, an antidepressant that had been prescribed to Mrs. Murrow. The doctors estimated that she had swallowed the pills around midnight, Christmas Day. It had taken six or seven hours for the drug to be fully absorbed into Jayne's system and for her to lapse into a coma. She was discovered unconscious around eight-thirty the next morning and rushed by ambulance to the emergency room at McKay-Davis hospital. Though her stomach was pumped, it was without hope. By that time nothing could be done but wait for the drug to silence her heart.

Mrs. Murrow had long suffered from bouts of clinical depression. Her illness was somewhat cyclical, usually rearing its ugly head around winter, lasting two or three months of each year. As lonely and isolated as she felt in her depression, she was far from being alone. Depression is among the most common of all humanity's plagues. It is also among the most misunderstood of all illnesses. Throughout history it has been called a hundred different things and attributed to as many causes, from evil spirits to Freudian concepts of conflict to recent discoveries of biological, genetic, and chemical origin.

Whatever else it may be, depression is a box of lies. The person trapped in this darkness often is unable to see past its murk to future happiness or even to past joys. They believe, erroneously, that they have always been unhappy and, therefore, always will be.

This trap is especially effective in fooling the young, like Jayne, who find themselves facing new pressures of life burdened with the intensity of powerful, new emotions. Without the benefit of life experience to keep these pressures in perspective, they often fail to see that the day will come when they will look back on the crisis they are currently facing and wonder why it all seemed too much to bear. No wonder so many young turn to the false and addictive escapes of drugs, alcohol, and sex. And some just give up and choose death.

Though our understanding of depression has changed, the one thing that hasn't changed is the stigma attached to it, and the blame and shame those suffering from it often take upon themselves. Mrs. Murrow had gone to great lengths to conceal her disease from her friends and society in general. And, as far as it was possible, herself. She did not want to believe that her daughter also suffered from the illness, though Jayne clearly manifested the signs. Mrs. Murrow took Jayne's death the hardest of all of us; quietly, but intensely punishing herself for refusing to recognize in her daughter what she had worked so hard to conceal in herself.

Unlike her husband, who hid his grief beneath his usual mask of stoicism, Mrs. Murrow wore hers where all could see. The first few days after Jayne's death she cried on every shoulder offered and laid her pain on as many backs as might help to carry it. Then her grief turned inward. She complained of severe migraines and sequestered herself in her darkened bedroom while the world flowed around her. We all feared, with cause, that she might need to be committed to a mental hospital.

Jayne had left a note. It was four pages long in handwriting that devolved from clear, structured script to a barely legible scrawl as the drugs took their toll. She apologized to her mother for the difficulty she had caused her and hoped that she would feel better not having to worry about her. She apologized for stealing her pills and had left money in a drawer upstairs to replace them. She apologized to her father for her bad grades and for dropping calculus. She apologized to Faye and Abigail for leaving them and said that she would miss them most of all. She apologized for being who she was.

She tried to write of the pain she felt, then abandoned the attempt with a matter-of-fact acceptance, as if that was just the way her life was and her decision was a rational one. The last thing she wrote was, "When there's only one door you eventually have to walk through it."

I believed that I had failed Jayne. Not intentionally. I would have stepped in front of a truck for her. But in agreeing to keep our conversation confidential, I had likely done more harm than good. Things couldn't have turned out worse than they did.

While I struggled with my failure, Faye was certain of hers. She knew it to the core of her being. She was the big sister. She had watched over Jayne at the passages of her life, from her first day in grade school to her first prom date. But when Jayne needed her most, Faye wasn't there. At least that's the way she saw it.

Not surprisingly, Faye did not tell her parents about her pregnancy. It had been relegated so far back in both our minds that I assumed that Faye had completely forgotten about it until the incident with the pills. The day of Jayne's funeral, Dr. Murrow gave Faye and his wife Valium. Mrs. Murrow took hers immediately. Faye secretly pocketed hers.

There was a family vigil the night before the funeral. The service was held in the

same church we had just days earlier attended for midnight mass, though it didn't
seem to be the same building—as if some
spell of circumstance had changed it
somehow, diminishing the splendor of the
very stone and wood of the edifice.

It was a somber occasion. Condolences
were mouthed, but more times than not
were awkward. Though I stood by Faye's
side the entire evening, I could not help but
feel she wasn't there. A part of Faye was
lost that moment in the hospital and what
remained was numb, bathed in the psychological anesthetic required for emotional
survival.

The funeral was held the following
noon. It was the second-to-last day of the
year. The sun mourned the day, buried beneath a pall of clouds that stretched across
the sky in a gray, leaden ceiling. The crowd
of mourners, especially Jayne's friends,
beautiful young people, some of them deal-
ing with their first taste of mortality, stood
around like huddled witnesses of some
great calamity, left breathless by its after-
math, like the people you see on news clips

standing around after a tornado has blown through their neighborhood.

The grave site was bitter cold. The chill did not envelop the mourners, but permeated them. Still, even a blizzard would have been welcomed, I thought, anything to breathe animation into such bleakness. Maybe funerals are, by definition, bleak. But none are so dismal as those for the young. Especially those young who forsake their own future.

I was asked to be a pallbearer along with five other men, all surnamed Thorup, members of Mrs. Murrow's family. As we laid the walnut casket on the stainless steel casket lowering device, I heard Faye begin to sob. Along with the other pallbearers, I unpinned my boutonniere and set it atop the casket. Then I went to Faye's side and held her. It is possible that it was the worst thing I have ever experienced. I don't know how anyone gets over it. Maybe they don't. One thing I was certain of, the only closure that day was the lid of Jayne's casket.

CHAPTER NINETEEN
Back to School

*In the face of the lies told
by depression, we must have
courage to survive. And courage
is best fed by hope. The sun will
rise again. The only uncertainty
is whether or not we will be there
to greet it.*

MICHAEL KEDDINGTON'S JOURNAL

Faye flew back to Baltimore just four days after her sister's funeral. A psychiatrist friend of her father had recommended a prompt return to her former routine—to cling to some driftwood of seeming normalcy lest she drown in grief.

The dean of student affairs called Faye in and they discussed the pros and cons of her taking a temporary leave of absence. They decided, at least for the time being, that it was best for her to stay on. Faye did not know or even wonder how her roommates knew about Jayne, but they did, and they were good to her. Lou Dean had a better heart than she let on. In a way, she became Faye's guardian angel.

I also went back to school. Winter quarter at Weber started January third. While my professors ran through their class syllabi, discussing course requirements, texts, and exam dates, my heart and mind were elsewhere. I thought only of when the best time would be for me to leave for Baltimore. I knew I had to be with her.

Helen had left on vacation two days after Christmas and did not return until the end of the first week of January. I cornered her in her office the day she returned. Her desk was piled high with paperwork accumulated in her absence. Not that such clutter was unusual. Helen's desk was always a mess. I once noted, to her dismay, that her trash can was the tidiest place in her office. Helen despised bureaucracy and its requisite paperwork. She once told me that her idea of a good workday was one when she went into her office just long enough to leave.

Though she had been out, Helen was aware of what had transpired in my life the previous week and had anticipated my request. "When do you want to go?" she asked.

"February sixteenth to the twentieth, Presidents' Day weekend. If I could take that Friday and the following Monday off, I could be back Tuesday for my shift."

Helen searched the surface of her desk until she came upon a red, loose-leaf binder containing a calendared schedule. She examined the schedule, though I suspected she had already decided to allow me whatever time I needed.

"We can swing that."

"Thanks," I said, standing.

She looked up over her glasses. "How's Faye doing?"

"Not too good. I can't imagine the pressure she's under. I wish I could do something for her."

"Seeing her will help."

"Maybe," I said.

"Why maybe?"

"I don't know. I wonder how much pressure our relationship adds."

"Why would it?"

I just shrugged. "I don't know," I lied. I stepped to the door. "Thanks for the furlough."

CHAPTER TWENTY
E.R.

Though adversity is the fertile soil in which the human spirit best grows, we loathe it still. I do not see how it can be otherwise, for no rational being seeks out pain and misfortune. Still, I cannot help but wonder if it is not somehow wrong to enjoy the fruit but curse the tree.

MICHAEL KEDDINGTON'S JOURNAL

The next two weeks were as uneventful as late-night television. I phoned Faye two or three times a day, just to speak to her once, if at all. Her schedule had changed and it was difficult to catch her in her dorm, though I did not really believe that her schedule was the culprit. I suspected that Faye was subconsciously avoiding me, along with all else that reminded her of her pain. As I had alluded to Helen, I added my own baggage to Faye's life, and as unwilling a porter as I was, there was no way around it.

As difficult as these times were, I did not begrudge Faye her neglect of me or our relationship. In the last four months she had been through more than anyone should have to go through. I worried about her, constantly, though mostly in silence. I worried that in carrying such pressure, somewhere along the line something had to give. That something came the night of January 18. Faye woke from her sleep screaming.

Lou Dean jumped from her bed. "What's wrong, Faye?"

"I'm wet."

Lou Dean rubbed her eyes. "You wet the bed?"

"I think I'm bleeding."

Lou Dean found the light switch. Faye was sitting up in her bed holding her hands in the air. They were red with blood. Her skin was pale. Lou Dean bounded from her bed and went to Faye's side. She yelled for Angel and Marci as she took Faye by the arm. "Just lie back, honey. I'm going to get help. Are you in pain?"

"I'm cramping."

"Marci! Angel! Where are you two?!"

The two women appeared in the doorway, squinting from the light.

"Faye's bleeding. You two stay with her. I'm calling the hospital."

Both women came to Faye's side while Lou Dean ran out to make the call.

The Johns Hopkins Medical Center emergency room is less than fifty yards from the dorm, just kitty-corner across a grass-lined concrete walkway.

Lou Dean called the emergency room directly. The emergency dispatch handled the call as an internal hospital emergency and the hospital arrest team was notified. Within minutes, medical personnel began entering the dorm. The first to arrive was the leader of the team, a senior medicine resident, a lanky, redheaded man wearing hospital blues. Lou Dean met him in the dorm's hallway.

"This way. I think she's miscarrying," Lou Dean said.

"You're her roommate?"

"Yes."

"Med student?"

"First year."

He followed her into the room, crouched by the side of Faye's bed. "You're pregnant?"

"Yes."

"How far along?"

"Twenty weeks."

He touched her arm. Her skin was cool and moist. A nursing supervisor and a surgery resident entered the room. The medicine resident said to the nurse, "Call E.R. Let's get a stretcher and some hands to carry her over." He visually checked her bleeding. The bloodstain on the sheet below her was about two feet square. He checked her blood pressure, then her pulse. "Low blood pressure, rapid pulse." The final member of the arrest team, the anesthesiology resident, arrived, followed by another nurse and a resident pushing a stretcher. The men lifted Faye onto it. Lou Dean took her hand and walked alongside her. "I'm with you, Faye. Everything will be okay."

The E.R. physician was standing at the emergency entrance to receive the stretcher. Lou Dean said to him, "I'm her roommate. We're both med students. May I stay with her?"

He looked at Faye. "Sorry, not now."

Lou Dean stepped back from the gurney

as it was pulled from the floor into a separate room. An oxygen tube was placed below Faye's nose. Faye's hand rested on her own forehead, partially covering her eyes from the harsh lights. The doctor gently touched Faye's shoulder. "Hello, Faye. I'm Dr. Liang. Do you know how far along your pregnancy is?"

"Twenty weeks."

"Are you feeling any pain right now?"

"I'm cramping."

He nodded, as if he had anticipated her response. He turned to the nurse who was now at Faye's side. "Get me two large-caliber IVs. We'll need lab work, coag and crit. Also a type and crossmatch."

"Will she need a transfusion?"

"Maybe. Not yet." He turned back to Faye and began reciting a checklist. "Are you on any medications or allergic to any drug?"

"No."

"Before now, has your pregnancy had any complications?"

"It's all been complicated," Faye said.

He smiled understandingly. "Any *physical* complications?"

"No."

The nurse brought over an IV needle. The doctor said, "You're still bleeding. We're going to give you some fluid. You'll feel two short sticks."

The nurse pushed a needle into Faye's arm, then taped it in place. She then inserted a second needle and taped it as well.

"You okay?"

Faye nodded. He placed both of his hands on her stomach, pressing down around her navel, confirming Faye's progression. "About twenty weeks."

A nurse attached the adhesive sensors of a cardiac monitor to Faye's chest while the doctor pressed his stethoscope to Faye's abdomen. He moved it around several times as if searching for something that eluded him.

"Anything?" a nurse asked.

"I'm going to need a Doppler. How's her vitals?"

"Stable."

A nurse handed him the Doppler and he placed its bell-shaped monitor on Faye's belly. He slowly moved it around, hunting for a fetal heartbeat.

"Do you hear anything?" Faye asked.

His forehead wrinkled. "Not yet."

He put the Doppler aside and started a vaginal exam. "Cervix is open. There's tissue," he said under his breath. "She's actively miscarrying. Call labor and delivery and let them know we'll be bringing a patient upstairs."

Faye's fatigue and anxiety spun the doctor's voice into babble.

"Go see if her roommate's still in the lobby," the doctor said. "Have her meet us at the elevator." He crouched by Faye's side. "Faye, I'm sorry, but your baby has died. We can't stop the bleeding without inducing labor. In just a few minutes a nurse will be taking you upstairs to deliver your baby."

"You can't take my baby," Faye said.

He answered gently but firmly, "Your baby's already gone, Faye. We need to stop the bleeding."

Faye began to cry, turning her head from side to side. "Just let me bleed. I should bleed."

His voice fell stern. "Faye, this isn't your fault."

Faye sobbed quietly. She covered her eyes with her hand. A nurse came to her side. "Is there someone you would like me to call before I take you upstairs?" she asked.

"No one," Faye said. "Please don't tell anyone."

It was around three in the afternoon that my phone rang. I was lying on my mattress reading. I stretched for the receiver. "Hello."

At first the only sound I heard was an ambient announcement over the hospital's PA system. Then Faye's voice came, frail and lifeless.

"Hello, Michael."

"Faye? Where are you?"

"At the hospital."

I guessed from her voice that her current whereabouts were not part of her training. "What's wrong?"

I could hear her sniffle. "I lost our baby."

Her words struck me like a blow to my chest. "Are you okay?"

"Yes."

"What went wrong?"

"We don't know yet."

A cold tremor swept through me. I could not bear to see Faye carry another burden alone. "Faye, I'm coming out."

"No, Michael. Don't come." There was something alien about her voice that troubled me.

"But why?"

"I don't want you here."

CHAPTER TWENTY-ONE
The Drive

The last few days have been a marathon. I have seen more of America in three days than in my previous twenty-three years.

MICHAEL KEDDINGTON'S JOURNAL

The day was a fraud, wearing a facade of sunshine and blue skies over crystalline blankets of snow. I was eating a bowl of cereal, reading a book I had bought to give to Faye, C. S. Lewis's *A Grief Observed*. I had one leg draped over the worn, corduroy arm of the La-Z-Boy recliner when the doorbell rang. I opened the door to find a uniformed Federal Express courier standing on my porch. He was holding one of their large letter envelopes. "I have a package for Michael Keddington."

"That's me."

He handed me a clipboard. "Sign right here, sir."

I signed his form and he relinquished the envelope. As the door shut, I glanced down at the mailing label. It was from Baltimore. It was from Faye. I went back to my couch and tore back the envelope's pull tab. Inside was a small, monarch-size envelope and a letter. I unfolded the letter. It was handwritten on Johns Hopkins Hospital stationery.

My dearest Michael,

I don't know where to begin. Or how to end. How to end us. My world has been turned upside down since we married. I don't know why God has thought to pour such pain into my life. I have considered that He is angry at me for not wanting my baby. I can't stand the guilt, the pain, the secrets, or the pressure any longer. I'm sorry, Michael. Please somehow forgive me. I will always love you.

Faye

My heart froze. I frantically tore open the small envelope. As I did so, Faye's emerald engagement ring fell to the ground. It bounced off the shag carpet and beneath the recliner. I fell to my knees to find it. It was there that the weight of her letter hit me. I stayed on the floor for a half hour.

Despite Faye's letter, it did not take much thought to decide my course. The first airline I called had a flight out at five. Then I got the price. Without advance booking, the fare for coach was more than thirteen hundred dollars. The other airlines were the same. I began packing my car.

I gathered a laundry bag of clean clothes, a box of Cap'n Crunch cereal, a bag of potato chips, a loaf of bread I had just bought, and an empty plastic milk jug that I filled with water, and threw them in the backseat of my car. I checked for tire chains in my trunk, then went back inside, lowered the thermostat, and locked my house.

I stopped by the bank and withdrew two hundred dollars, drove to the Chevron near the freeway entrance and topped off the Datsun, bought a gallon of wiper fluid and a Rand McNally map of the U.S.

With a felt-tipped pen I drew a route from Ogden to Baltimore, a nearly straight line along I-80 for more than two thousand miles. I folded the map back to expose the first leg of my journey and clipped it to my visor. Then I cleared my odometer and started my journey.

An hour and a half later I crossed the Wyoming border at Evanston. I made a brief stop in Rock Springs at someplace called Cruel Jack's Travel Plaza, then continued east on I-80 through Rawlins, Laramie, and then to my birthplace, Cheyenne. I had not been back to Cheyenne since I was thirteen, when my mother and I fled our life in Wyoming in an ancient Chevrolet station wagon. I filled my tank, then bought a couple tacos at Taco John's. I had planned to spend the night in Cheyenne, but the ghosts forced me on. I drove an hour more, over the Nebraska border, and stopped at a motel in a small town called Ogallala.

I slept uneasily. I woke the next day by six, grabbed a danish and a carton of milk at the gas station while I topped off my tank, then headed out. I arrived in Omaha shortly before eleven, stopping only for gas and a drink. Around one I reached Des Moines. I was fatigued and stiff and allowed myself the luxury of a sit-down lunch at a Burger King and a fifteen-minute catnap before setting off again. I stopped in Davenport for gas and reached Gary, Indiana, as the winter sun began to fall below the horizon in my rearview mirror. I thought of my mother. She had loved *The Music Man* and I had grown up to her scratched record of the musical playing on the phonograph. *Gary, Indiana, Gary, Indiana, Gary, Indiana.*

I stopped an hour later in South Bend to spend the night at a roadside motel I fondly called "the Bates." Every fiber of fabric in the room reeked of tobacco, as did I by morning. The last time I felt so queasy was when I was nine and my mother caught me out behind the house smoking one of my father's Marlboros. Her punishment was to make me finish the rest of the pack under her torturous glare. My mother understood behavior better than B. F. Skinner and Pavlov combined. I never smoked again.

I took a shower, though it was no more pleasant than the rest of my experience. The motel's plumbing had its own will and the water's temperature fluctuated somewhere between frostbite and scalding. I fled the place, stopping at an on-ramp McDonald's for a breakfast sandwich, and was on the road by seven. I stopped for gas just outside of Toledo and again in Youngstown, Ohio. Though the roads were clear, the best I had experienced on the three days, there was frequent road construction and the traffic became steadily more dense as I left 80 at the 76 junction, following it south to 70 and all the way down into Maryland. I arrived in Baltimore at the beginning of rush hour.

CHAPTER TWENTY-TWO
The Reunion

Though we pay homage to the gods of intellect and reason, in the end we believe what we want to believe.

MICHAEL KEDDINGTON'S JOURNAL

In retrospect, I suppose that it was odd that I had no anxiety about our reunion. I had confidence that I could set things right if I could only see Faye and talk to her. In truth, I was more anxious about my car making the trip. I felt like Charles Lindbergh. I had covered more than twenty-one hundred miles in two and a half days in a twelve-year-old Datsun B210. It was like crossing the Atlantic in a hang glider.

With the assistance of a clerk at a Krispy Kreme doughnut shop I found the medical center. It was less than a half-hour drive north of downtown Baltimore. It was only as I pulled into the hospital's parking lot that the first twinges of anxiety danced in my stomach, suggesting the possibility that I had done the wrong thing in coming. Faye had not said, "Don't come." She had said, "I don't want you here." It was not a subtle difference. Perhaps it wasn't confidence that drove me two thousand plus miles; perhaps it was desperation.

I knew from previous conversations with Faye that Reed Hall was only across the walk from the hospital. I grabbed a clean shirt from the backseat and changed from the sweat-stained one I wore. I pulled on my coat, locked my car, and walked to the dorm.

It was deceptively cold out, the air laced with chilling humidity.

Reed Hall was a flat-faced, nine-story building of red brick, dwarfed by the hospital in whose shadow it fell. I walked in through a glass entryway opening to a large security counter where residents and guests were required to check in. A large black woman sat at the desk. She was wearing a gray coat with a badge. Standing behind her, talking on a handheld radio, was a smaller, bald man. He wore no coat, but there was an embroidered security badge on his shirt's sleeve.

"May I help you?" the woman asked.

"I'm here to see Faye Murrow."

"Is she expecting you?"

"No, ma'am."

"What's your name?"

"Michael Keddington."

She thumbed through an index then lifted her phone and punched at a keypad. "Miss Murrow please." She listened for a moment, thanked someone, then hung up. "Miss Murrow is not in. Would you like to leave a message?"

I glanced to either side of the counter. To my left was a small sitting area with chairs and a couch.

"Thank you, no, I'll just wait for her." I started to walk toward the lounge.

"Sir, you're not allowed past the desk," she said. "Not without a resident."

I stopped.

"That's the regulation."

I could see from her demeanor that there was no talking her out of it. "I'll go outside and wait."

Twilight began to descend, dragging the temperature down with it. I sat on one of the benches that flanked the entryway for about an hour, until the cold became unbearable and I went for a walk to warm up. I walked toward a large, gable-roofed building with a large dome on top. A sign out front designated it as the administration building. Inside its entryway was a large statue of Jesus Christ. I had seen the statue before, at least a replica of it. When I was ten my mother and I had gone to Salt Lake City to see the Christmas lights on Temple Square. I had seen the sculpture inside the glass atrium of the visitor center there. My mother stopped and looked at it for a long while. I was cold and bored and wanted to leave. When I finally turned her from the statue with my whining, there were tears in her eyes. I did not understand her tears, but I somehow knew they were different from other tears and that I was not to be afraid of them.

I wandered around the building for about forty-five minutes before I returned to the dorm. In my absence there had been a change of shift and there was now a tall, gray-haired woman sitting alone at the desk. She rang Faye's room for me, but Faye still had not returned. I asked her if I could wait inside, but she evoked the same regulation and with equal fervor. I went back out to the bench to wait.

The butterflies I had felt in anticipation of seeing Faye had long since flown and were now replaced with the subtle gnawing of hunger. I realized I had not eaten since breakfast in South Bend, which already seemed like a week ago.

I was about to go off to find some dinner when Faye finally walked by. She was by herself. Her backpack was slung over one shoulder and her eyes were distant, as if her mind pursued other paths than the one she slowly walked.

I called out to her. "Faye."

She did not seem to hear me at first, still deeply immersed in thought. Then she casually glanced over. Her expression turned to one of disbelief. She stared at me more as if she had seen an apparition than her lover.

"Michael? What are you doing here?"

I stood up. "Hi."

"What are you doing here?" she repeated.

I had had three days to rehearse this moment in my mind, though I suddenly felt none the better prepared for it. I stepped toward her, reaching into my pocket as I did. I brought out her ring, holding it in the palm of my hand. "I brought this back."

She looked at the ring but made no move toward it or me. I couldn't read her expression. I took another step forward. "Take it."

She eyed me warily, as if I were a stranger offering her candy. Then she asked, "Why are you doing this?"

Her question baffled me. "Doing what?"

"Why did you come?"

"What kind of question is that?"

Three women walked by and Faye turned slightly sideways. "Didn't you read my letter?"

"Of course I did. That's why I'm here."

"It's over, Michael."

Her words cut. "How can it be over? We haven't even talked."

"I don't want to talk." She suddenly turned and began to walk toward the dorm. I pursued her in, past the security desk. The guard placed me with Faye and waved me in as I passed. Faye pushed the elevator UP button.

"Come here, Faye." She didn't respond. "Just let me hold you."

Her face reddened in exasperation. "It's all holding me, Michael. If you read my letter, you didn't understand it. It has nothing to do with you or how we feel about each other. Those things are irrelevant."

"How can they be irrelevant?"

She raised both hands. "I can't do this. I just can't." A bell rang and the elevator door opened. She stepped in and I followed her. She did not look at me as she pushed the fourth-floor button.

"We can make it through this."

She faced the elevator door. "Maybe you can, but I can't." The elevator bell rang again. The door slid open and she stepped out.

"Faye."

She walked just a few yards to her apartment, pulled out a key, unlocked the door, then stepped partially inside, blocking the entrance to the room with her body. "I'm sorry, Michael, but I can't give you something I haven't got. We never should have gotten married." She shut the door, leaving her words ringing in my ears like a gunshot. I hit the door with my fist. "Faye, I'm not leaving until we talk."

She didn't respond. I pounded the door still harder. Another door, just a few yards to my left, opened. A bemused face peered out at me, then the door shut.

"Just give me a half hour. I drove three days to get here."

Her voice came muffled and pained. "Please, Michael, just go."

"Faye, open up!" I shouted.

Just then, from the other end of the hallway a uniformed security guard approached. His voice was tight and stern. "Sir, step away from the door."

I glanced at him dismissively, then pounded again on Faye's door. "Open up, Faye."

There was still no reply.

"You can't just walk away from this like nothing happened."

The security guard stepped up to me. He was roughly my size, a little older, a little broader in the shoulders than I, but with a stomach that hung over his black leather belt. He spoke more threateningly. "I said, step away from the door."

I turned on him angrily. "This is none of your business. Leave us alone."

"Don't see *us,*" he said. "I just see *you* harassing one of our residents. You can leave on your own or in handcuffs."

"I'm not leaving until I finish what I came for." I pounded again on Faye's door. "Come on, Faye. Open up."

At that the guard reached for my arm. I snatched it back from him. He stepped toward me and my temper flared; I swung wildly at him. Though I missed, he stumbled backward and fell. He turned crimson with rage. He lifted his radio from a belt clip and yelled into it, "Mark! Get up here!" He pulled a wooden baton from his belt.

Within moments another guard, slightly larger than the first, with a more muscular build, stepped from the elevator. He saw his associate's drawn baton and pulled his own from his side as he swaggered toward me. As I anticipated his approach, the first guard lunged at me, shoving me up against the wall. As we wrestled, the other guard snapped me across the back of my neck with his stick. I fell forward, wincing with pain. Both men jumped me, pressing me to the ground. My jacket was pulled up around my head as one of the guards tried to lock my arms in a full nelson. Most of the doors in the hallway had opened to investigate the commotion and we now had an audience of female spectators.

Suddenly the door in front of us opened. Faye stood in the doorway. At first she was uncomprehending, confused by the tangle of men at her feet. Then she gasped and lunged forward, grabbing the arm of the man on top of me in an attempt to peel him off.

"Get off of him! Leave him alone!" She began pummeling the guard with her fists. The men were surprised by Faye's sudden intervention. The first guard grabbed Faye by the wrists to stop her assault on his companion.

"Let go of me!" she shouted, struggling to pull her hands free.

"Take it easy, ma'am."

"Get off of him! What are you doing? He didn't do anything wrong."

The three of us stopped struggling. Red-faced and breathing heavily we turned to face her.

"You know this man?" the first guard asked.

"Yes, he's . . ."

Faye paused, and in a strange twist of the dramatic we all—the guards, myself, the voyeurs peering down the hallway—stared at her in anticipation.

"Who am I, Faye?" I prodded.

With red eyes, Faye gazed at me for a moment, then said, ". . . an old friend."

Her words struck harder than the baton had. For a moment we were all still, then I shook my arm loose from the guard's relaxed grip. "An old friend," I repeated. I crawled up to my knees, then to my feet. My shirt was torn and a thin stream of blood trickled from my nose. Ironically, of all the spectators that lined the hall, I felt sympathy only from the guards, if not for my rejection, then for the humiliation.

I looked once more at Faye, but my eyes were beginning to burn and there was nothing more to say anyway. I wiped the blood from my nose. Then I took the ring from my finger and tossed it at Faye's feet. I turned away and stumbled down the hallway to the elevator, followed only by the faint commentary of the women. I left for home.

CHAPTER TWENTY-THREE
An Empty Bed

*The drowning man is not
picky about which lifeboat
he climbs into.*

MICHAEL KEDDINGTON'S JOURNAL

The drive home took a day longer than the drive out. It felt like a year longer. Faye had broken my heart and pieces of it were strewn two thousand miles across America.

From Nebraska I called Helen for the first time since my flight. I had left her shorthanded, forcing her to take two of my shifts herself. She wasn't happy, though she seemed somewhat relieved to hear from me. She patiently heard me out before she launched into the obligatory employer's reprimand, though we both knew that her heart wasn't in it. I told her I'd be back at work by the next shift if I still had a job waiting for me. She assured me that I did.

I arrived in Ogden at three in the morning of the twenty-sixth, wired from colas, coffee, and caffeine pills. I turned the thermostat back up above sixty, wrapped myself in a wool blanket, then dropped fully dressed onto my mattress. Despite the stimulants, I fell asleep within minutes, the accumulated exhaustion of the week's marathon finally catching up with me. I slept for more than twelve hours straight, waking at three-thirty that afternoon. Just in time for work.

I was in a dark mood. I was never much good at hiding my emotions, and that night, for the most part, everyone kept their distance. Only Sharon asked if I was okay. I apologized to her for the inconvenience my disappearance had caused her, but she didn't seem too put out.

An hour into the shift I was reviewing the daily report when I noticed that Blythe's grandfather was absent from our resident list. I asked Sharon where he was. She frowned. She was not happy to be the bearer of more bad news.

"He passed away the night before last," she said.

"What happened?"

"He had a second stroke and threw a clot."

"Were you with him?"

"No, his granddaughter was. She rang us, but it happened fast. By the time I got to the room he was gone."

"How did she take it?"

"She was pretty broken up. She asked about you. Wanted to know when you'd be back."

"What did you tell her?"

"I told her I didn't know."

"Do we still have his resident sheet?"

"It's in the outpatient file; that's in the gray file cabinet in Helen's office. Do you know where the key is?"

I nodded. Helen's office was locked, but she always left her key in the planter outside her door. I found Blythe's phone number on the residence sheet and dialed it, but no one answered. I went back to my rounds. Though my heart was heavier, the news tempered the darkness of my mood with my concern for Blythe.

About a half hour before the end of my shift, I noticed a woman walking toward me from the far end of the east corridor. She was obscured by the hall's darkness and, at first glance, I thought it was a resident, as she shuffled a little, her head slightly bowed. As she approached I realized it was Blythe.

I walked to her and put my arms around her. She lay her head onto my shoulder. "I'm sorry," I said. She began to cry. I don't know how long I held her. It was a while. It was as if she had held in all her grief for my return. When she could speak she said, "The doctors told me it might happen. I just didn't want to believe it."

I didn't reply, but held her tighter.

"I wish that you were here when he went. It would have been easier on him. It would have made it easier on me."

I started to apologize but she stopped me.

"You don't owe me an apology. You don't

owe me anything. That was meant to be a compliment. Okay?"

We stepped apart. Her nose and eyes were red. She reached into a sweater pocket and dabbed at her cheeks with a wadded tissue. "Don't look at me. I'm a mess."

I felt helpless, seeing her in such pain. "What can I do?" I asked.

"I don't want to be alone right now."

"I'm off work soon. We could get a coffee or something."

She lowered her head. "I know I'm selfish to ask that of you. You've been driving all week. You're probably exhausted."

"I'm okay. I slept until three this afternoon. I don't want to be alone either. No one's in the dayroom downstairs. Why don't you just rest awhile. I'll get you when I'm off."

"Okay."

I walked her over to the elevator, hugged her again, then went back to finish my final rounds. I clocked out at midnight and went to the dayroom, which was dark except for the dancing projections cast from the television. Blythe lay across the couch, watching an old black-and-white movie. Despite my assurance that the room was vacant, she wasn't alone. On the couch opposite, one of the female residents snored.

"Aren't there enough beds?"

I smiled at the question. "Melva won't sleep in her own room. Are you ready?"

She yawned, then stood up. She seemed a little unsteady on her feet.

"Maybe I should just drive you home," I said.

She shook her head sleepily. "No. I don't want to go home. My mother's there."

CHAPTER TWENTY-FOUR

The Pancake House

Rarely do we invest the time to open the book of another's life. When we do, we are usually surprised to find its cover so misleading and its reviews so flawed.

MICHAEL KEDDINGTON'S JOURNAL

My windshield was iced over, so Blythe waited in her car with the heater on while I scraped my windows, then dusted the snow off of hers. We drove separately to the Denny's on the corner of Twenty-fourth and Harrison. When I met her in the parking lot she already seemed to be feeling a little better. The restaurant was surprisingly busy for the hour, a peculiar mingling of truck drivers, college students, and goth teens.

Our waitress led us to a corner booth, handed us our menus, then returned a moment later with ice water and an order pad. I ordered chamomile tea, then decided it would likely put me to sleep, so I ordered a large Coke instead. Blythe ordered hot chocolate with extra whipped cream. The waitress returned quickly with our drinks and our check. Blythe stirred the cream into her chocolate until it turned milky with a thin, white froth.

"You look like you're feeling a little better," I said.

"It was hard going back there. I'm sorry I unloaded on you like that. I just realized how much I wanted to see you. I guess I've depended on you through this. I don't have anyone else." She took my hand. "How are you doing?"

"All right," I lied.

"Really?" She clearly didn't believe me.

I hesitated. "No. Not really. I feel like a train wreck. Did anyone tell you where I went?"

"Sharon said you drove back east, but that's it. She was tight-lipped about it. I figured you'd gone to see Faye."

I nodded.

"It didn't go well?"

"No."

"What happened?"

"She wants to end us."

"I'm sorry," Blythe said. After a moment she added, "If it's any consolation, your marriage lasted three months longer than mine." She slowly spun the porcelain mug between her fingers. "I never told you about it, did I?"

"No."

"His name was Travis." She paused. "Sounds like a country singer."

"There are at least a hundred country singers named Travis," I said.

She smiled wryly. "Travis had had this girlfriend since middle school. They'd practically grown up together. After twelve years of dating she decided it was time to move on and she found someone else. I was in the wrong place at the right time. I was his rebound. Six months later we were married." She fidgeted with her spoon. "I guess I had it coming. What do they say, 'eyes wide shut'? I knew that he still wanted her, I just didn't want to be-lieve it. I finally got the courage to ask him about her, he said that he had drained that tub. I knew he was lying. What was he sup-posed to say? 'I married you because she didn't want me'? I told myself that he would get over her." Blythe scratched her forehead. "It's amazing how easy it is to lie to ourselves when we really want something. I guess we both were liars."

"You loved him?"

"I thought I did. Whatever that means. Last week in my interpersonal communications class someone read an article that said love is a reaction of the pituitary. Researchers say that when the pituitary is removed, like from cancer or something, that person never feels that whirlwind, head-over-heels feeling of love." She raised then lowered the cup from her lips. "What do you think of that?"

"I think you're getting loopy," I said.

"I am." She smiled. "And I think I could have used a pituitary-ectomy years ago. I'm bad at love. I just throw my heart up like a skeet target to see if anyone wants to blow it into a million pieces."

"Did your pituitary love him?"

She averted her gaze, and this time her answer was softer. "I loved him. I would have been good to him. I understood about his girlfriend, how he could still want her. I would have taken him back if he'd wanted to come back. I guess I was just lucky that it ended when it did. Before our lives became more entangled. You know, with children."

"So he went back to her?"

"One phone call from her and he went crawling back. No, he went flying back. All the way to San Diego. I thought he was on a business trip. He spent a weekend with her before he bothered to call and tell me that we were through. I could hear her laughing in the background. I don't think she was laughing at me, probably watching television or something, but she might as well have been. It added to the moment. It was the most humiliating experience of my life."

I frowned empathetically. "I can sympathize. I had a *real* memorable one this last week in Baltimore. I was assaulted by the security guards when I tried to see Faye. In front of an audience of female med students."

"They assaulted you?"

"The guards, not the women."

She laughed. "I figured."

"I guess I started it. I took a swing at one of the guards."

She again smiled wryly. "I can still outdo you. Get this. He asked for the engagement ring back."

"You didn't give it back to him?"

"I may be naive, but I'm not stupid. I pawned it. I bought my grandfather a color television set. It was the best thing that came from the relationship. At least the most lasting."

"Tell me about your grandfather."

Her demeanor suddenly changed, and for a moment I was afraid I had done the wrong thing in opening that door. Instead I realized that she held those memories close, where she could get at them. She was glad for the chance to bring them out and dust them off.

"He was really wonderful. We used to walk together every morning. He would carry a bottle of salt with him. There was an apple tree along our walk where there were these really great green apples, you know, the tart kind, and we would sit by that tree and salt apples and laugh." She was suddenly lost in fond remembrance and an endearing smile crossed her face. "He was an angel. I don't know how his kids got so screwed up, but he never let me down. He attended all those things my mother should have but didn't. Dance recitals. Teacher conferences. My graduation. He gave me away at my wedding." She grinned. "I told him that if he shaved his legs he could be my bridesmaid.

"I thought he was going to hunt down Travis and bring his head back on a platter when he broke off our marriage. He would have if I had let him. He couldn't stand to see me hurt." Her eyes began to moisten. I reached across the table and took her hand. "Everyone should have someone in their life like that."

"What about your father?"

"I don't know anything about him. I don't know if my mother does either. I'm sure she was drunk when I was conceived."

"I'm surprised you're not more bitter toward men."

"I went there for a while. But my grandfather kind of ruined it for me. My best
friends have always been men."

I glanced down at my watch.

"Are you ready to go?" she asked.

"No. Why?"

"You looked at your watch."

"I was just wondering if it's too early for
breakfast."

"Men plan their lives by their stomachs."

"You say that like there were another
way."

She looked suddenly thoughtful. "It is really late. I better let you go."

I realized that I did not want to go, that I
received as much comfort from her as she
did from me. Maybe it was her, maybe it
was just a sympathetic heart, but we had
one thing in common Faye and I never had.
Neither of us had anyone else. The thought
of leaving Blythe tonight was suddenly unbearable.

"We could go to my place," I said.

Her green eyes blinked in surprise, then
she smiled. "All right."

At that hour there were no other cars on

the street as Blythe followed me down the snow-packed roads to my house. We went inside. I turned on a lamp, took Blythe's coat, then put my things in my room. When I came back out Blythe stood before two framed photographs mounted on the wall. "Is this your mother?"

"Yes."

"She's very beautiful." I sat down on the couch, waiting for her to comment on the portrait next to it. "Faye?" she said simply.

"Yes."

She turned to me. "Your place is nice. Very masculine."

"Masculine. That's a polite way of saying chaotic."

A wry smile curved her lips. "Maybe." She came over and sat on the opposite end of the couch. It was nearly four and fatigue was kicking in like a drug. We just looked at each other for a moment; she moved over closer, then into me, laying her head against my chest. "How about I sleep right here?" she said. She lifted her chin and kissed me lightly. When I did not resist, she pressed her lips more tightly against mine and reached up and started to unbutton my shirt. I placed my hand on hers, stopping her. She pulled back and looked at me quizzically and blushed. "I'm sorry, I thought . . ."

I raised her hand to my lips and gently kissed it. "I don't want to be alone either. But I'm still married."

She looked at me almost disbelievingly. "I can't believe she let you go."

She glanced down at her hand cradled in mine, then back up into my eyes. "Would you just hold me then?"

I pulled her into me, wrapping my arms around her back. Her hair was fragrant and soft against my face. I raised my hand and caressed the straw yellow strands that fell between my fingers.

I had once been told in confidence by a minister that the greatest challenge and temptation he faced was that in following the biblical admonition to comfort those who mourned, to not become emotionally attached to those vulnerable hearts he touched. At that moment I understood perfectly what he had meant. I was filled with love, desire, guilt, and longing for two women—one who owned me but no longer wanted me, and the other who wanted me but could not have me. At least not yet.

There was another emotion, a shameful, vindictive one, that danced briefly in the darker wings of my mind. A part of me wanted to take Blythe, not for Blythe's sake, but for Faye's, to match her betrayal. I quickly pulled the curtain on the thought.

I held Blythe, and her breathing evolved into a smooth rhythmic fall and her arms loosened around me as she fell asleep. I closed my eyes. And I dreamt of Faye.

I awoke at dawn lying next to Blythe. Her head still lay against my chest, and though she could not see my face, she knew from my stirring that I was awake. She said softly, "I'm in love with you, Mr. Keddington. I've been in love with you for some time."

I didn't reply.

She looked up at me and found my eyes. "I know, it's still new. You'll hurt over her. But I'll wait. And I'll comfort you."

I wrapped my arms tightly around her, then kissed the top of her head. She cuddled back into me. About ten minutes later she lifted herself. "We're both late for school." She got up, went to my bathroom, then returned. "Look at my hair," she laughed. She tugged at an errant strand. "Bed head," I said, smiling. I retrieved her coat and we met at the door. We kissed at length.

She looked into my eyes and a broad smile spread across her face. "Will you call me tonight?"

"Definitely."

CHAPTER TWENTY-FIVE
Flight

So often the pain of our life is no more than a reminder to take our hand off the stove.

MICHAEL KEDDINGTON'S JOURNAL

Faye delayed filing divorce papers, knowing that the mechanics of a divorce do not release one from the pressure of a relationship, rather they intensify it. At this point that was more pressure than Faye could handle. As our marriage had already run on autopilot for five months, she felt no driving compulsion to bring it to a conclusion.

Faye's delay did not lead me to believe there was hope of our reunion. Not after Baltimore. Our relationship had not been cleanly severed, rather it had been yanked apart, leaving frayed ends and seemingly no means to reattach them even if the will to do so had been there. And on Faye's end there clearly wasn't. On my end I was no longer certain.

The human mind, like nature, abhors a vacuum, and with the sudden absence of all that had preoccupied her thoughts, Faye focused her mind on her schoolwork. Ironically she was learning the art of healing the body in order to avoid the more difficult and relevant course of healing the heart and the soul.

There was perhaps one exception to her isolation. Faye found herself frequently thinking about Hallie and her little girl. She did not know why; whether it was a manifestation of the truism that misery loves company or if it was something more specific—if the loss of her own child reminded her of a woman struggling against hope to hold on to hers. No matter the reason, she knew she had to see her.

It was late Friday afternoon and Lou Dean put her arm around Faye as they walked from their last class of the week.

"I know what we're doing tonight, girl-friend, and it ain't homework. There's a party down at South Point with plenty of anesthetics and hot boys. The noncommittal kind. Just what you need right now."

"I don't need hot boys," Faye said.

"Well, you definitely could use the anesthetics."

"I already have plans," Faye said.

"Sure you do."

"There's someone I need to see."

Lou Dean stopped walking and eyed Faye skeptically. "Who?"

"A friend."

"What friend?"

"She's the waitress from Canelli's."

"Huh?"

"The one who served us that night the four of us went. You know, the one who dropped the tray of drinks?"

"Are you lying to me?"

"No."

"What's her name?" she quizzed.

"Hallie."

"No," Lou Dean said, "it was Judy."

Faye looked down, unwilling to explain the situation.

Lou Dean put her arm back around her.

"Look, I just don't want to find you sitting alone in the dorm feeling sorry for yourself. No one has more right to it than you do, but it will eat you up. But you do what you need to do."

"Thanks," Faye said.

Lou Dean gave her a quick hug. "All right, hon. I'll see you later. Would you mind taking these back to the room for me?" She held her books out to Faye.

"Sure."

The women parted and Faye returned alone to the dorm. The apartment was quiet and dim. Only the light in the kitchen was on, reflecting off the cinder block wall of the hallway. Faye set down her things then walked into the kitchen. Marci was there, alone, sitting at the table. To her side was an inkwell of stone. Marci held a long, wooden pen resembling a brush, and her hand moved down a sheet of paper in fluid strokes.

"Hi," Faye said.

Marci looked up. "Hello, Faye."

"Where's Angel?"

"She is at the library." Marci went back to her writing.

Faye opened the refrigerator and poured herself a glass of iced tea, then sat down next to Marci. She studied the beautiful Mandarin characters on the page in amazement. They bore more resemblance to painting than writing. "It's like art," Faye said.

"I am writing to my husband and son."

Faye took a sip of her iced tea.

"How did you get the name Marci?"

"My English teacher at Beijing University gave us names. In Chinese our last name is spoken first. My family name is Ma. It means horse. My given name is Syi. It means hope. So my Chinese name is Ma Syi. My English teacher was an American. He thought my name sounded like Marci."

Faye thought about it. "You are a long way from Kansas."

Marci cocked her head.

Faye smiled. "When was the last time you saw your family?"

Marci set down her pen. "It has been seven months."

"When will you see them again?"

"When I finish school."

Faye looked at her incredulously. "But that's nearly four years."

She nodded.

"Can't you go back?"

"I cannot afford to go back."

"How can you be away from them for so long?"

"I do it for my husband and my son. I am very fortunate. I scored very high on a government test. Many women do not have any school at all. They have to be prostitute to support their family. It is a good and honorable thing to be a doctor. I can help my village and many people. And I can give a good life for my son."

Faye smiled darkly. "You come here and give up so much to help everyone you love and all I have done is let everyone I love down."

There was silence.

Marci looked at Faye, then said timidly, "May I speak of your sister?"

Faye looked at her curiously. "Yes."

"Your sister had depression?"

"Yes."

"We learn about depression. It is an illness. I do not understand your culture, to make mental disease different than body disease. If your sister die of cancer you do not blame yourself. But if she die of depression you think it is your fault."

Faye looked at her darkly. "I never said it was my fault."

"To yourself, you say this. And you punish yourself. You have changed in many ways. You no longer talk to your boyfriend, but I think you still love him. Maybe you are not so unlike your sister and you also choose not to live."

Faye looked down, covering her eyes with her hand.

"I am sorry if I said something wrong."

Faye abruptly stood and went to her room. She shut the door and lay down on her bed, closing her eyes. When she opened them again it was dark outside. She checked her watch; it was late, almost nine. Marci was gone, and Faye was alone in the apartment. She pulled on her coat and went outside. Along the wet, moon-drenched street she walked four blocks to Canelli's.

It was ladies' night at Canelli's and the pizzeria was crowded and raucous. Faye descended the stairs, which were crowded with loitering teenagers, and walked in. Craig, the night manager, stood behind the cash register at the front counter. He eyed Faye lecherously as she approached, then reached for a menu.

"The lovely lady is dining alone tonight? Or were you thinking of finding a takeout?" He flashed an oily grin.

"Is Hallie," she caught herself, "I mean, is Judy here?"

"No, Judy's out tonight. Will I do?"

"Will you do what?" Faye asked icily.

Craig abandoned his attempt at flirtation. "Judy quit a few days ago."

"Quit?"

"Didn't even bother to call."

Faye couldn't imagine any scenario in which Hallie would quit. Unless the police had found her. Panic surged through Faye. Without another word, she turned and hurried to the door. She climbed the stairway to the sidewalk and hailed a cab. A blue and white taxi pulled up to the curb and Faye climbed inside. The driver was Jamaican and his black, braided hair fell below his shoulders. A red, yellow, and green Rasta ribbon hung from the rearview mirror, along with two pictures: one of Bob Marley and the other of the driver and three small, dark-skinned children, two boys and a girl. The syncopated rhythm of reggae pounded from a cassette player mounted below the car's dashboard.

"I need to go to the corner of Mason and Green Street."

The driver picked up a map and began searching for the streets. Faye said, "I'll tell you how to get there. It's not far from here."

"Okay, Missy, you show me the way." The driver pulled a U-turn and headed south toward Hallie's neighborhood. As the car turned down Green Street the driver looked over his shoulder at Faye. "This is not a safe place, Missy."

"I know," Faye said. As on Faye's previous visit, the street and house were dark, but the snow had mostly melted, surviving only in an occasional muddy patch, leaving the street gray and ugly. The cab stopped at the house and Faye handed the driver his fare. "Would you mind waiting here a minute. There might not be anyone home."

"Don't look like nobody home, Missy," he said. "You be careful. I'll wait."

Faye stepped across a swath of brown, damp lawn and walked to the side of the home and descended the stairs. She knocked on the door. There was no answer but the hollow echo of the stairwell. She pounded again. She waited several minutes, then put her ear to the door. The cabdriver honked. Faye reluctantly climbed the stairs and began walking back to the car. As she reached for the cab's door she heard a low voice call after her, "Faye?"

She turned back. Through the darkness she could see the silhouette of a head peering over the concrete wall of the stairwell. Faye thanked the driver then walked back. Hallie met her at the top of the stairs and threw her arms around her.

She wore an oversized sweatshirt with the Canelli's logo and denim jeans that fell short of her ankles, exposing Teva sandals and thick socks.

"I didn't think I'd see you again."

"Of course I came back," Faye said.

Faye followed her back to the apartment. As they descended the darkened stairs, Faye thought that Hallie moved more stiffly than she had remembered. They entered the apartment and Hallie shut and chained the door behind them.

In the room's dim light Hallie looked sick. Frailer than before. Her skin was wan and there were deep wells beneath her eyes. Sarah was lying on the mattress, wearing an oversized T-shirt for a nightgown. She looked up when she saw Faye.

"Hi, Sarah."

"Howdy, Aunt Faye."

Hallie smiled. "We read a cowboy story tonight." She motioned toward the table. "Let's sit over here. Not that there's anyplace else to sit."

Faye noticed two upright suitcases in the corner of the room as she walked to the table.

"I'm sorry I didn't answer the door right

away," Hallie said softly. "I thought you
might be the police."

Faye took off her coat. "I just came from
Canelli's. The manager, what's-his-name,
said you just stopped coming in."

"Craig," Hallie said, frowning. "Things
have gotten worse."

"Your MS?"

Hallie glanced over at Sarah and fell
silent. The child's eyes were still open and
she was intently trying to hear what the
women were saying. "You liked the toys
that Aunt Faye brought, didn't you?" Hallie
said. Faye turned around.

"Thank you, Aunt Faye."

"You're welcome, sweetie."

"She was so happy Christmas morning.
She asked if she could make you a card."
Hallie walked over and retrieved a piece of
paper from the top of the refrigerator and
handed it to Faye. It was a crayon drawing
of a purple Christmas tree. There was a
stick figure of a woman with brown hair
standing next to a smaller figure.

"That's you and me by a Christmas tree,"
Sarah said.

"It looks just like us."

"Now go to sleep, honey," Hallie said. Sarah quickly ducked under the cover like a rabbit disappearing into its hole. Hallie walked over and knelt next to her. She stayed there until Sarah fell asleep. She then returned to the table, answering Faye's earlier question as if there had not been an interruption of their conversation. "My MS is always getting worse. It's not that."

Hallie's face stiffened, and she closed her eyes tightly, blinking back the tears that still seeped through. Faye reached across the table and took her hand. "What is it?"

Hallie wiped her eyes. "Last Tuesday I was working late. My last table had just left. The cooks were back in the kitchen scrubbing down the grills. Sarah was asleep in the booth. I was up front. Craig came out of the back. He started touching me. When I tried to resist he pushed me up against the counter. I lost it. I told him I'd had enough of his harassment and that I was going to call the police if he didn't stop. He just laughed. He said he'd thought of calling the police himself. He said that he had a friend at the police station and he could have a background check done on me. He said he thought the police might be interested in my little girl." Hallie started to cry. "He knew he had me. He started groping me. I just shut my eyes. He made me say that I owed him after all he's done for me. I actually said it, that I owed him. I was so afraid."

Faye spoke slowly, controlling her anger. "What has he supposedly done for you?"

"For giving me the job without asking questions. And for letting me hide Sarah at the restaurant. He said that, 'hide her.' I don't know how he figured it out. He said he usually had higher standards for his women, but he'd lower them in my case. He said we were going out on a date Sunday night after work and he better not be disappointed. He just smiled the whole time. I didn't know what to do. I've been hiding ever since."

Hallie looked at Faye helplessly. "I keep

wondering why God is doing this to me. Just when I think things can't get any worse they do." She started to cry. "What am I going to do? Where are we going to live? I was lucky to find this apartment for so cheap. My landlord didn't even require a deposit or first month's rent. I have less than two hundred dollars left. My MS has gotten so much worse in the last year. I don't know how I can start over." She dropped her head in her hands. "And I'm just so tired. Every cell in my body is tired. I can't go on anymore but I can't stop. What would happen to Sarah?" She looked at Faye, her eyes weary and dim. "I feel like Job. It's like God is trying to break me. It's like He's only given me one door to walk through."

Her words fell into silence though they echoed loudly in Faye's mind. Faye said softly, "That's what my sister wrote." She looked into Hallie's eyes. "When I was home for Christmas she committed suicide."

Hallie's mouth opened. "Oh, Lord."

Faye lowered her head. "Then I lost my baby."

"I am so sorry," Hallie said.

"And I sent my husband away with the rest of my life. I guess I'm like you in a way. I'm just running. Except I don't know what I'm running from."

The women sat in silence. Hallie looked even more weary, as if the burden of Faye's trials had been added to her own. Finally Faye said, "It's late. You need to sleep."

"I'll call you a cab. I can use the phone upstairs."

"Don't worry about me. Let me help you." Faye helped her up and walked her over to the mattress. Hallie lay down on it next to Sarah as Faye pulled the blanket up around the two of them.

"How will you get home?"

"I'll be okay."

Hallie closed her eyes and within just a few minutes she was asleep. Faye went and sat in the corner of the room next to the lamp. Then she reached over to the lamp and turned it off and sat in the darkness and thought.

CHAPTER TWENTY-SIX
Another Door

There would be less suffering in this world if humanity would learn this one truth: It is not what we receive but what we give that heals us.

MICHAEL KEDDINGTON'S JOURNAL

When Faye awoke she was lying on the floor, her coat wadded up and her head resting on it. The sun broke through the back window of the apartment, backlighting Hallie, who stood at the kitchen counter. Hallie had heard Faye stirring.

"Good morning."

Faye groaned and rubbed her face. "What time is it?"

"A little after eleven."

Faye pushed herself up to a sitting position.

"I didn't know if I was supposed to wake you," Hallie said. "I'm sorry if I was."

"No. I don't have school today." Faye had never been in the apartment during the day. The light from the window well made the room seem less dismal. "Where's Sarah?"

"She's in the backyard trying to make a snowman. It snowed a little last night. Are you hungry?"

"No. I don't eat breakfast."

"I was thinking lunch," Hallie said, smiling. Hallie spooned herself a bowl of oatmeal from a pot on the hot plate and brought it over to the table. She did not look as sick as she had the night before. Faye realized that her frail appearance last night was likely less a result of her chronic illness than the unrelenting stress of her life.

"I was surprised to find you still here," Hallie said.

"I was up pretty late. Actually all night. I was still up at dawn."

"Doing what?"

"Thinking about you, mostly. And your situation."

Hallie said, "Where did your thoughts take you?"

Faye stood and walked over to the table and sat down next to Hallie. "I wondered why you're in my life at all. I've probably met ten thousand waitresses in my lifetime and I don't remember a single one of them. Except for you." Faye's voice was soft and thoughtful. "I'm not into fatalism. At least I don't think I am. I listen to my Chinese roommates talk about fate and meeting each other and I think it's about as meaningful as a fortune cookie. But sometimes I think there might be something to it. I don't believe that we're meant to go through this life alone. I believe that God puts people along our path." Faye sighed. "You said something last night about God giving you only one way out. I think you're wrong. I know Jayne was wrong. There's always more than one door. I believe we resist the solution, because we can't see it from our vantage point, but it's there. We're like the bird that gets caught in a house and keeps flying into the glass window when if it would just move a few feet to one side it would find an open door. There's always a way. But sometimes we need to trust in others to show us." Their eyes met. Faye's voice turned. "You need to go home, Hallie.

You need to go to where someone can take care of you."

Hallie frowned. "You know I can't do that, Faye. You know that. They'll take her."

"No, they won't."

"I can't take that chance."

"They won't, Hallie, because *I'll* take her."

Hallie gazed at her in disbelief. "You'll take her where?"

"No one would ever look for Sarah in Ogden, Utah. She would be safe with me until you're sure she can come back."

"But you're in school."

Faye didn't answer.

"You can't quit, Faye. I won't let you."

"What choice do we have?" Faye lowered her head. When she spoke again her voice was strong and resolute. "In the last month I've lost my sister, my baby, and my husband. And for what? I've buried myself in school and I honestly don't know why. It seems that all the assumptions I've based my life on haven't gotten me anywhere but lost. Maybe God placed me here right now because I'm the only one in the world who can help you. If not me, then who?" Hallie couldn't answer. Faye's voice cracked. "And maybe in helping you and Sarah, I can find my way back too." Faye slid her hand across the table until it covered Hallie's. "Could you trust me with Sarah?"

Hallie looked down, then toward the door. She couldn't speak.

CHAPTER TWENTY-SEVEN
The Second Reunion

I have wondered what I would say if I ever saw Faye again. No longer.

MICHAEL KEDDINGTON'S JOURNAL

Though I didn't usually work Saturdays, my reckless flight to Baltimore had left me with a list of favors to return. I worked at the Arcadia until midnight Friday night then was back by seven to work until one. Early that morning as I slept, a winter storm moved in and by noon had already dropped eleven inches of snow; it still fell relentlessly. Blythe and I had arranged to meet at my house after I got off work. She was going to take me snowshoeing somewhere up in the canyons.

My feelings for Blythe were growing, filling in the cracks of my broken heart. Blythe was spontaneous and joyful. She had a refreshing acceptance of life for what it was, instead of what it could be.

Blythe was kind and good and open in her
love for me. We had much in common, the
two of us, more perhaps than Faye and
I ever had, for life had dealt us similar
cards. So why was I so confused? And why
did I still pine for a woman who no longer
loved me?

A half hour before noon I was paged to a
phone call.

"Hello, this is Michael."

"Where's my daughter?" a voice bel-
lowed.

"Who is this?"

"You know damn well who this is.
Where's Faye?!"

Only then did I know who it was: the
only man I had ever allowed to speak to me
like that. And I realized that I would never
allow him to do so again. I was free of him.
It was excruciatingly liberating.

"What are you talking about?"

"You know what I'm talking about. She
packed up and left school last night."

His words stunned me, but my surprise
was suddenly replaced by anger. "I don't
know where she is. What's more, I don't

care." I hung up on him. As satisfying as it should have been, I took no pleasure in it. I had lied. I wondered about Faye and where she had gone.

When I arrived home there were two cars in my driveway: Blythe's dark brown Monte Carlo and a car I had never seen before, a fire-engine red Pontiac Grand Prix. The snowplows had been by, narrowing the street in their wake and raising drifts on the curbs as high as three feet, closing off several of my neighbors' driveways. I guessed that one of the neighbors had parked in my drive. I pulled my car in behind Blythe's and walked up to her. She rolled down her window at my approach.

"Hi," I said.

She smiled. "Hi. How was work?"

"Long and over," I said. "At least until Monday."

"Do you have someone staying with you?"

"No, I think that's just one of the neighbors' cars."

"Because when I pulled in, someone peeked out from behind your curtains."

I looked at my house. "You saw someone inside?"

She saw my surprise and her face suddenly mirrored my concern. "I couldn't see who it was. Should we call the police?"

Just then I realized whose car it was in my driveway. "No. Just a moment."

I walked up to the front door. As I suspected, it was unlocked. I brushed the snow from my hair and shoulders, then stepped inside. "Faye!"

She emerged from the darkened hallway leading to my bedroom. We just stared at each other, neither of us sure of what to say.

"What are you doing here?"

She looked at me, uncertain. "I'm sorry. I had no place else to go. I thought maybe we could talk."

Her choice of words angered me. "I drove two thousand miles to talk to you. You didn't want to talk then. Was it an inconvenient time?"

She bowed her head in response to my

sarcasm. "I'm sorry," she said contritely. "I am so sorry."

"Don't you think it's a little late for apologies?"

She looked up at me and tears began to well up in her eyes. "If you say it is."

We were both silent. Just then a small girl emerged from the shadows behind her. "Faye, I'm thirsty."

Faye looked down at her. "Just a minute, honey."

"Why are you crying?" the little girl asked.

Faye crouched down next to her. "Go through that door. I'll be there in just a moment to get you some water."

The child furtively glanced up at me then darted off through the kitchen door. I looked to Faye for an explanation.

"I'm looking after her. Do you mind if I get her a drink?"

"Of course not."

She walked to the kitchen. The two of them emerged a few moments later and Faye led her to the bathroom, then came back out to the front room alone. "Her name is Sarah. I dropped out of school to take care of her. Her mother is very sick and her father is abusive."

I didn't know what to say. It was an even odder twist to an already surreal moment. Just then there was a quick knock on the door and Blythe stepped in. "Michael? Are you . . ." She froze at the sight of Faye.

I looked between the two of them. I could see the hurt in Faye's eyes and the apprehension in Blythe's. To Blythe, Faye had taken on an almost mythical importance—someone who played a significant role in Blythe's future, yet she had never expected to actually meet.

"Faye, this is Blythe."

"Hello," Blythe said awkwardly.

Faye didn't respond. There was the sound of the toilet flushing, then the little girl returned to the room. Blythe looked down at the child quizzically. Faye said, "Get your bag, Sarah."

The little girl again disappeared. Faye looked at Blythe, then back at me, her eyes dark with pain. "She's pretty. It didn't take you much time."

"I don't think you're in any place to pass judgment, Faye."

The little girl timidly walked into the living room carrying her bag. Faye took her hand. "C'mon, honey."

Without a word, Blythe stepped to the side of the door. Faye stopped a few feet from her and looked Blythe directly in the eyes. Then she looked back at me. "You're right, Michael. I'm sorry." She turned to Blythe. "I'm sorry."

Faye walked out to her car, buckled in her little ward, and drove away.

CHAPTER TWENTY-EIGHT
Ginny

Oftentimes, only in standing alone do we keep from falling.

MICHAEL KEDDINGTON'S JOURNAL

No one at the Murrow home saw Faye pull into the driveway. She set the parking brake, unbuckled Sarah, and lifted her out. She held the child's hand as they walked up to the gabled front porch, opened the door, and stepped into the dark foyer. The house was still. Faye looked into the den and living room and found both rooms vacant. Then she walked down the hall to the kitchen.

Dr. Murrow sat at the oval kitchen table over a calculator and a clutter of check stubs and bills. He looked up at her and his eyes flashed with anger. Faye suddenly felt very small, like a little girl about to be punished. Sarah stood in front of Faye with Faye's hands resting on her shoulders.

"What are you doing here?" His voice was harsh and grating.

Faye swallowed, steeling herself against the fear she had always felt of her father's anger. "I quit school."

"You quit." His lips lifted in an incredulous smile. "Just like that you quit medical school," he said, as if reciting the punch line of a joke. He looked down at Sarah. "And who is this?"

"Her name is Sarah. I'm taking care of her."

"You're baby-sitting?" he said sarcastically.

"She's the daughter of a friend of mine in Baltimore. Her mother is very sick and needed my help. So I took her."

"You quit school to baby-sit someone's child?" He glowered. "You're just full of surprises. Anything else? Join a cult?"

Just then Abigail walked into the room. "Faye!"

"Out, Abigail," her father said.

Abigail stood confused. "But I want to see Faye."

"Now!" he barked. Abigail recoiled and

slunk back down the hall. Dr. Murrow turned his attention back to Faye.

"Her father abused her. He has AIDS, Dad, but the court won't protect her. So her mother ran away with her. But she's sick and she can't run anymore."

"This child was kidnapped? Oh, this just keeps getting better." He shook his head. "You're abetting a felon! Do you realize how serious that is? You could go to jail. Not that any of this would surprise me at this point." He walked over and lifted the phone. "I'm going to call Ken at Family Services. He'll know what to do with her."

"Don't, Dad."

Her father exploded. "This is not a stray puppy, Faye! I don't know what kind of game you think you're playing!"

"Game?! Is that what this is to you? I think it's you that's playing a game. Our whole life has been a game. Play by these rules, pass GO, collect two hundred dollars."

He stared back at her, astonished.

"Why are you a doctor? So you could drive a nice car and have a bigger home than everyone else? Is that how you play your game? Why do you want me to be a doctor? So you can brag to your friends? Is that part of the game too, Dad?" Faye wiped her eyes with the back of her hand. "You should be proud of me. I've given up my dream to save a child's life. Isn't that what a hero would do? What more did you want from your daughter? Because if this life is only a game to see who gets the highest position or the most education or the most money, then it was never worth playing. Just ask Jayne, Dad."

Faye began to sob. Dr. Murrow was speechless. Sarah stood wide-eyed and trembling. When Faye regained her composure, her eyes were dark and her voice came hard and sharp. "If you call your friend, I'll run. And you won't see me again until Sarah's grown and gone."

Dr. Murrow slowly set the phone down. Only then did he notice his wife standing in the doorway on the opposite end of the kitchen. "Ginny?"

Faye glanced over. Neither knew how long Mrs. Murrow had been standing there.

She looked haggard, aged and pale. Her hair was matted. She was barefoot and wore a flannel nightgown. Faye had never before seen her mother like this and it frightened her. Mrs. Murrow did not acknowledge her husband, but looked at Faye. "Welcome home, dear," she said gently. Then she glanced down at Sarah. She slowly walked forward and crouched down in front of the little girl. She delicately touched Sarah's cheeks.

"Hello."

Sarah did not answer but gazed on shyly.

"What's your name, honey?"

"Sarah, ma'am."

"Welcome to our home, Sarah."

There was flat silence in the room. Dr. Murrow spoke again. "Ginny . . ."

Before he could finish, Mrs. Murrow turned back and the look in her eyes silenced him. "This child needs us, Ben." She stood and squarely faced her husband, her jaw tight; her eyes, like her voice, were strong and clear. "And I am not going to lose another daughter."

CHAPTER TWENTY-NINE

An Unexpected Visit

Life, like a good book, often comes full circle.

MICHAEL KEDDINGTON'S JOURNAL

My confrontation with Faye had left Blythe and me stranded in an emotional no-man's-land—one we escaped by strapping snow-shoes to our feet and trudging through four feet of snow up Ogden Canyon, near Snow Basin. It was growing dark as we returned, the shadows falling, painting the day's conclusion in purple twilight.

We were both exhausted and kicked off our boots outside my door. Once inside I had started a fire and Blythe sat on the sofa in front of the hearth while I made a pot of hot chocolate in the kitchen. Neither of us had said much about Faye's return, though Blythe seemed as affected by it as I. Maybe more so. I suppose we feared to stir the coals lest a fire leap from them.

It was night when a silver Cadillac Coupe DeVille parked in my driveway. A minute later there was a knock at my front door. I answered the door to find Dr. Murrow standing on my porch. As usual, he was dressed in business attire; gray wool slacks beneath a long black overcoat parted to reveal a navy-and-yellow striped silk tie. He had left his car idling, its exhaust visible in the cold air: obviously he intended to make a speedy getaway.

As quickly as I had opened the door, I began to shut it on him. He reached out his hand to stop me. "Please," he said. His voice was neither harsh nor forceful. There was a quality to it I had not heard before.

"Just let me speak my piece, then I'll leave you alone. Forever if you like."

I did not shut the door, tacitly agreeing to hear him out.

He took a deep breath and I saw the anxiety in his face.

"Faye doesn't know I'm here," he started. "She came home today. I know you know that. She told me that she came over here. She told Ginny and me everything. About the two of you eloping, the baby, about your trip to Baltimore."

I steeled myself for whatever tirade he might be planning. To my amazement, there was no evidence of rancor in his eyes, only sadness.

"You know I haven't cared much for you. Not because of anything you've done. From everything I've ever heard, you've always been good to my Faye. But I wanted more for my daughter. At least what I thought was more. The thing is, Faye loves you more than anyone."

He hesitated again. He blinked, then turned away, not wanting me to see the pain in them. I wondered what possibly could have forced him so humbly to my door.

Still I said nothing.

"I guess this is my point. The world has fallen in on my little girl. Just remember that."

I suddenly understood. It was not the arrogant chief surgeon nor the posturing millionaire making this request, it was a father who loved his child. For the first time since I had met him he was willing to set aside his own prejudice and pride to speak on behalf of his daughter. For once he was seeking to exercise not his will, but hers. I never would have believed it possible.

Dr. Murrow hesitantly moved his hand forward, as if unsure whether or not to shake mine, then he withdrew it and tipped his head slightly. "Thank you for letting me speak." He turned and walked the ice-slicked cement path back to his car.

I shut the door behind him, astonished by the encounter. I turned to Blythe, but she was no longer seated on the couch. I found her sitting at the kitchen table, her fingers laced around a cup of cocoa. She looked up at me sadly. "That was Faye's father?" she asked.

"Yes." I sat down across from her at the table. "Did you hear our conversation?"

"Some of it."

"I can't believe he came here," I said indignantly. "He's berated and ostracized me from the day we met. Now he wants me to take back his daughter. After what she did to me."

Blythe suddenly stood and walked back out to the living room. I followed her.

"What was that about?" I asked.

She was collecting her things, her back turned to me. "You still love her."

I was surprised by the accusation. "Did I miss something here? How'd you get that from what I just said?"

She spun around. "You don't need to say it, Michael."

"I *didn't* say it."

"No, you did. You just don't know it. You said it all afternoon with your silence. And you said it right now with your anger."

"Of course I'm angry. Why wouldn't I be?"

"The opposite of love isn't anger. It's indifference." She pulled on her coat. "I've been down this road. I'm not going to do this to myself again."

"Do what to yourself?"

Her voice was raw and hurt. "Love someone who's still in love with someone else."

In that moment I saw the truth of her accusation. Blythe turned and started to the door.

"Wait," I said.

She stopped but did not look back. "Don't do this to me, Michael. Please. Because if you ask me to stay I'll stay." Her voice softened and she slowly turned toward me. "If you can't tell me that you don't love her anymore, then let me go while I can."

I stood speechless. The seconds seemed stretched into minutes, but I couldn't say what she needed me to say. We both knew it would have been a lie. Finally Blythe looked down, raising a hand to wipe a tear from her cheek. Then she took a deep breath.

"I didn't think so," she said. She walked to the door and stepped into her unlaced boots. Then she paused at the threshold. "You know what's ironic, Michael? If you could have told me that you don't love her anymore, I think I would have lost what I love most about you."

I took a deep breath. "Can we keep in touch?" I asked.

As she gazed at me her eyes filled with tears. She walked back to me and kissed me gently on the cheek. "I don't think so. I care a little bit too much for you." She forced a smile. "See you around, handsome."

She turned and walked away, closing the door behind herself.

One of the sweetest women I had ever known had just walked out of my life. And the only honest and kind thing I could do was let her go.

CHAPTER THIRTY
The Twilight Carousel

I have come to believe that the defining moments of most lives are not acts of courage or greatness, rather they are the simple acts: expressions of virtue or vice that are tossed carelessly like seeds from a farmer's hand, leaving their fruits to be revealed at a future date. But not always. There are moments that are like some cosmic examination. And like all examinations, there are those who pass and those who fail.

MICHAEL KEDDINGTON'S JOURNAL

Clouds still blackened the night sky, their edges frayed and moonlit, rent in places to reveal a velvet, starlit sky. I pulled on my boots and parka and drove across town to the Murrow residence. Despite the hour, most of the home's lights still burned. Faye's rental car was not in the drive, though I considered that it might be in the garage or had already been returned. I knocked on the door. Dr. Murrow answered. His face was solemn and weary, but I sensed that he was pleased to see me. He said in a concerned voice, "I don't know where she is, Michael. I don't know where she'd go at this hour."

I can't explain how, but at that moment I knew exactly where she was. I got back in my car and drove to Summerset Park.

The park was closed, confirmed by a reflective sign posted out front. The large iron-pole gate that swung across the entrance was chained and padlocked. I was not surprised to see Faye's rental car parked against it. I pulled my car in behind hers, then hopped the concrete retaining wall and started to trudge through the thick snow to the park's west end. To the carousel.

The park was as still as a cemetery at dusk. The carousel was a hundred yards or more from the park entrance. The clouds had drifted southward and a full moon lit the ground, revealing a fresh set of footprints in its crystalline reflection. In the distance was the dark skeleton of a Ferris wheel. To the west of it was an iced-over pond, surrounded by a chain-link fence posted with Thin Ice warning signs. The fence continued to the boathouse, where the paddleboats were stacked upside down on top of each other like plastic cereal bowls in a cupboard, raised as high as the shack's eaves. As I approached the carousel I could see beneath a shadowed canopy of elm the shape of a park bench fused with Faye's faint silhouette. She sat motionless, her head bowed as if in prayer, as inanimate as the surrounding trees, more so, for even the elm occasionally swayed with an eastern wind. I remembered the last time Faye and I had been together at this park, on the very bench where she now sat; the warmth of the day, the sun glowing nearly as brightly as Faye's countenance, as brightly as the hope Faye had once had.

I walked slowly up to the back of the bench. My approach could not have surprised her. The shin-deep snow was crusted with ice and each step echoed through the silent park as if I were walking on broken glass.

"Faye," I said gently. She did not move. I leaned over the back of the bench. I could see the moonlight reflected off her tear-stained cheeks. I noticed that she clenched something tightly in her gloveless hands. I came around and sat down at the edge of the bench, still breathless from my trek through the deep snow.

"I thought I'd find you here." I glanced over to measure her response. Her eyes were tightly shut, keeping her thoughts sequestered deep inside herself. The silence stretched as clouds of breath froze before us. I looked ahead at the darkened carousel. It was closed for winter and its canvas walls were pulled down around it like a giant pillbox. I took another deep breath, the cold freezing my nostrils.

"It's like my dream, isn't it? The one I told you about the last time we were here."

Faye said nothing.

"I suppose we've had a few dreams since then. And we've seen a few of them die." Faye's eyes were still closed. "You know, people are always writing about carousels, like they're some great metaphor for life." I sniffed then rubbed my nose. "It's a pretty poor metaphor if you ask me.

"I guess we want to believe that life just

goes around with little ups and downs and when the ride's over, all that matters is that a good time was had by all. We want to believe we know what's around the next bend." I looked at her. "But life isn't that way. It wasn't that way when my father left my mother and me. Or when we lost our home and came to Utah. Or when my mother died. Or when Jayne died." I paused. "Or when our baby died."

Faye lowered her head into her hands.

"Life isn't like any carousel I have ever known. It's not that safe or predictable. We never know where or when someone's going to get off. There are no promises. The truth is, if we knew what the ride was like we probably would have just saved our ticket."

I looked back out across the naked winter landscape. "We can't even promise our time. It's not ours to give. The best we can promise is our hearts. And the most we can hope for is to live each moment so when it's all over, there are no regrets." I suddenly felt like I was talking to myself. I looked at Faye and it entered my mind that I might never sit this close to her again.

"I don't know where you are anymore. I don't know what you're thinking. I'm afraid of you. No one has ever hurt me as much as you have. No one else could have because I've never loved anyone so deeply." I looked down, rubbed my hands together, more from anxiety than cold. "Maybe I'm just not very good at letting go. But before I do, you should know this. I've never stopped loving you. Even when you tore my heart from my chest, it still beat for you. When I sent you away tonight, I cut myself with every word." My voice cracked.

"Faye, with everything I feel, I want you back. Whatever moments we may be blessed or cursed with on this ride, I want to take them with you."

Faye didn't move, didn't speak. Then her hands slowly opened, exposing what she had been holding. It was my gold wedding band. The one I had thrown at her feet in Baltimore. Faye suddenly began to cry, then she looked up at me, into me, with those beautiful fawnlike eyes that revealed everything she held in her heart.

"Oh, Michael, I hoped you would come for me."

This was a year that revealed all of our souls.

MICHAEL KEDDINGTON'S JOURNAL

Epilogue

Faye and I had a "real wedding," as Mrs. Murrow put it, on July eleventh of that year. The ceremony was at the Church of the Madeleine. Our reception was held at the Murrows' house. Dr. and Mrs. Murrow spared no expense. There were even peacocks in the yard. I didn't know you could rent peacocks. It was the most extravagant affair I had ever attended. There were likely a thousand people there and the guest list read like a Utah's *Who's Who*, including Ogden's mayor, a U.S. senator, two congressmen, and Utah's governor and first lady. Though I wished my mother could have been there, a part of me suspects she was. I felt her love around us. Faye's roommate Lou Dean came. She was loud and impertinent and we bonded instantly. Once a Wyomingite always a Wyomingite, I guess.

Abigail and a very pregnant Shandra were Faye's maids of honor. Sarah was the flower girl. Faye was luminous.

There was also a "real" honeymoon. As a wedding gift, the Murrows arranged a week-long vacation in Maui with a stay at a beachfront resort called the Grand Wailea. It was paradise—the kind of place I had seen on *Lifestyles of the Rich and Famous*, but did not think was accessible to mere mortals. Faye was more at home with it all. For me it was a long way from west Ogden.

Two weeks after we returned from our honeymoon, Faye and I moved to Baltimore. Faye had met with the dean of student affairs, and after explaining the circumstances of her going AWOL, Johns Hopkins granted her a leave of absence and the chance to start school again that August.

Dr. Murrow was good to us as well. He continued to finance Faye's education and agreed to pay for our apartment as well as "reasonable" living expenses. His generosity allowed me to go back to school. I doubt I'll ever call him Dad, but when we flew home for Christmas that year he patted me on the back and told me that I was a great son-in-law and that he was proud of me. Even though he'd drank a bit too much eggnog, I took his words in the spirit they were intended. Sometimes old age or liquor is the only way those walls come down in men.

Dr. Murrow arranged for Sarah to be examined at McKay-Davis. It was determined that she had, in fact, been sexually abused. Dr. Murrow's political clout came in handy. The governor blocked Sarah's return to her father in Alabama, and even though legal jurisdiction was in Montgomery, charges were filed against Sarah's father. He was never brought to court, though some said he was brought to justice. He died of PCP, an AIDS-related pneumonia, that August. In light of the new evidence, the child abduction charges that had been filed against Hallie were dropped within two weeks of his death.

Dr. and Mrs. Murrow had flown Hallie to Utah to be with Sarah. She stayed with them for nearly a year in Jayne's old room. Now that her days of running are over, Hallie has decided to stay in Utah. She resides in a two-bedroom apartment off Harrison Boulevard, just a few miles from the Murrows' home. She claims to have fallen in love with the beautiful mountains and temperate summers of Ogden, but I think she mostly just fell in love with the Murrows. Sarah calls Faye's mother Aunt Ginny and Abigail "big sister." Though Abigail has needed professional counseling to deal with Jayne's loss, she is resilient and is doing better every day. She is enjoying her role as a big sister.

I called Helen and she got Hallie a job doing clerical work at the Arcadia. Sharon is still there. Brent finally got the boot; I saw him last Christmas working a cash register at a convenience store.

A week after we moved to Baltimore, Faye took me to Canelli's to see where it all began. With the Murrows' assistance, Hallie had filed suit against Craig and the restaurant. In the end it was settled out of court for $45,000, enough to give Hallie a new start and a van equipped for her special needs. She is not yet in a wheelchair, but it is just a matter of time. Craig, of course, was fired and now carries a mark on his employment record as ugly as his own soul. His wife left him. I heard that his attorneys also left him—bankrupt. I have difficulty feeling much pity for him. There are none so deserving of justice as those who prey on the helpless. We don't know where he is. I suspect no one cares.

Hallie's MS continues to advance, but she is now receiving medication to slow the exasperations. And she can get the rest she needs.

We miss Utah and, conveniently, Faye has forgiven the University of Utah for dropping my scholarship. She now hopes to do her residency at the U of U med center. I'm sure she'll be accepted. Any institution would be lucky to have her. She will make a fine doctor someday.

I think of Blythe from time to time. I hope that she has found the happiness she deserves. I will always love her for her good heart and the comfort she brought me at a difficult time. I like to think that maybe I brought her some comfort too. But I don't know. I will forever consider myself in her debt.

Whenever I look back on the course of that year, I marvel at how many different paths came together and cannot help but wonder if there was not a greater hand in its design. Surely God is in the details.

Of course the sorrow we carry for Jayne will never leave us. On this front, Faye continues to fight battles, some in which I may join her and some in which I must stand helplessly by. But time brings healing, slow as it may seem in coming, even to our greatest losses. Not all stories have happy endings. But in this story, Faye and I are together and each day I thank God for that. And maybe that's the best anyone can hope for. Or should hope for. That's just the way life is off the carousel.

A Gift for My Readers

Over the years, I have received many requests
for a compilation of material from my works—
quotations, diary entries, and thoughts from
the characters who populate my novels.

I am pleased to now make available

THE QUOTABLE EVANS
*Diary Entries, Letters, and Lessons from
the novels of Richard Paul Evans*

To order a free copy, please e-mail me at:

www.richardpaulevans.com

or send your name and mailing address to:

Richard Paul Evans
P.O. Box 1416
Salt Lake City, UT 84110

Copies will be available as long as supplies last.
There is no charge for the booklet or the
shipping and handling.

Thank you for your continued interest
and support.

About the Author

Richard Paul Evans is the bestselling author of the *Christmas Box* trilogy and *The Locket*, as well as the children's books *The Dance*, *The Christmas Candle*, which received the 1998 American Mothers' Book Award, and *The Spyglass*. There are currently more than ten million copies of his books in print. All proceeds from Evans's books for children go to the Christmas Box House International, an organization that he founded, dedicated to building shelters and providing services for abused children. He lives in Salt Lake City, Utah, with his wife, Keri, and their five children. He is currently working on his next book.

Please send correspondence to Richard Paul Evans at:

P.O. Box 1416
Salt Lake City, UT 84110

Or visit his Web site at:

www.richardpaulevans.com

Richard Paul Evans is a nationally acclaimed speaker. To request Mr. Evans for speaking engagements, please fax your request to (801) 532-6358 or contact the above address or Web site.